SINFUL GAMES

A Checkmate Inc. Novel — Book 4

SHELLY ALEXANDER

ABOUT THE CHECKMATE INC. SERIES

Leo Foxx, Dex Moore, and Oz Strong spent their youths studying a chessboard, textbooks... and women, from afar. Now they're players in the city that never sleeps. Gone are their shy demeanors, replaced with muscle, style, and enough sex appeal to charm women of all ages, shapes, and cup sizes. They've got it all, including a multimillion-dollar business called Checkmate Inc.—a company they founded together right out of college.

Some guys are late bloomers, but once they hit their stride, they make up for lost time.

And the bonus? The founding partners of Checkmate Inc. didn't become successful and smokin' hot by accident. They were smart enough to surround themselves with guys who helped them transform into the men they are today. So get ready for more stories about the hotties who are connected to Checkmate Inc.

A fun, flirty, and dirty contemporary series of STANDALONE novels in which the sizzling hot players associated with Checkmate Inc. meet their matches.

ALSO BY

DEDICATION

For the love of my life. You were my inspiration years ago when I was first inspired to write my own love stories, and you're still my inspiration today. I love you with all my heart.

PROLOGUE

"She made the first move, so I'm all in and ready to play."
—*Oscar (Oz) Strong*

Sometimes life gets fucked up. Is it my fault?

Usually.

I might be a literal genius in biochemistry, completing multiple degrees in the time it takes most people to finish one. I might have made the right choice when I let two of my college chess team buddies talk me into putting my multiple degrees to work in an unexpected way that has made us ridiculously wealthy. I may be the founding partner who developed our full line of wildly success- ful, supercharged pheromone colognes, which literally fly off the shelves and send men flocking to one of our worldwide retail studios where we focus on improving the whole man for a hefty five-figure fee. I might've even been damned smart coming up with the idea to take our multimillion-dollar company, Checkmate Inc., public.

But that doesn't mean I make the most intelligent decisions when it comes to my personal life.

For instance, I let my parents push me into marriage right after I finished at Columbia. They meant well. In their own way. They honestly believed persuading me to marry inside of our family's *economic class* would make me happy. I was young, green, and gullible as hell, so I agreed to the introduction, the rushed engagement, and the six-figure wedding at The Plaza.

I should've reminded my dear old mom and dad that their geekster, brainiac son had spent a lot of time at the gym over the years packing on muscle, and I had also learned how to treat a lady both in and out of the bedroom. Sure, I'd have left out the part about how well I know my way around a woman's body, but my point is...I'm not a bad catch. With an IQ of one hundred eighty-four, I've been doing chemical equations and coefficients since the age of five, so I'm smart enough to run a successful company, as well as pick my own woman.

But *naw.*

I married a girl because my parents liked her family's name. A girl who didn't love me but loved my parents' old money and their seven-thousand-square-foot *cottage* in the Hamptons because she'd grown up in the same tax bracket.

A girl who fucked me over by fucking the entire male membership at our country club. Her idea of fun was to get down and dirty with her Jiu Jitsu instructor—who had the IQ of a rock and couldn't pay his own bills—just to see how the other half lives. Her words, not mine. No idea why she's still with the twit.

Thank you, Jill. And good riddance. Divorcing her was the best decision I ever made, besides following my business partners to Manhattan to start Checkmate Inc.

I'm also man enough to admit that I actually believed the carpet burns on Jill's knees, ass, and back were from Pilates.

Smart people really can be obtuse to the point of idiocy.

Which is why falling for my new assistant at the height of the #metoo movement wasn't only my biggest fuck up, but was also a mistake that could put both of my business partners and our company's future at risk.

I just can't help myself, though. There's something about this girl that I can't get out of my mind or my fantasies. I can't stop wondering what she feels like or what she tastes like.

What she sounds like when she's in the throes of a window-shattering orgasm.

It's stupid, I know. But then she goes and makes the first move, and fierce competitor that I am, I can't help but rise to the challenge.

I'm all in and ready to play by her rules. I just don't realize until it's too late that the game she wants to play is seductive, steamy, and sexy. Oh, and so positively sinful.

CHAPTER ONE

"You're fired," I growl from behind my desk at the assistant sent over this morning from the temp agency.

The young man's face crumples as he gathers up his things and hurries out of my office, sniffling at the Checkmate Inc. logo etched into the glass door. My gaze snags on that logo—the knight, my favorite piece on the chessboard.

Since the outer facing walls on the executive floor of our head-quarters building in Manhattan are all glass, I can see my former assistant jerk his man-purse from the desk just outside of my office, then he breaks into a run in the direction of the elevators, wiping his eyes.

Fuck.

I'm going to catch hell for this. Not from Human Resources, because hell, I'm *their* boss and can fire them as easily as I just canned the temp. No, it's my two business partners who won't let me hear the end of it once they find out I've let another assistant go.

I take off my Armani glasses—the only remaining evidence of my former chess team nerd status—and rub my eyes.

Hanging onto the glasses was a pact I made with my college-chess-teammates-turned business-partners so we'd never forget our roots and the risk we took on each other to start this company. Keeping the glasses wasn't a problem for me because I never gave a shit about looking like a brainiac nerd. The geekster persona kept gold-digging friends and fake girls from sniffing around because of my trust fund—mostly.

The nerdy frames are gone, though, replaced by stylish designer brands and a wardrobe fit for a king. Hell, even a pair of the jeans my personal Checkmate Lifestyle Coach picks out for me at our anchor retail studio on Fifth Avenue costs as much as a small country.

But the outward transformation was a must because of the nature of our business—improving the *whole* man from the inside out.

If our clients only knew the expensive wardrobe and two-hundred-dollar haircut were an exterior mask that hides the irreparable damage caused by my previous marriage. My young heart was crushed into dust, and my emotions turned to stone. Which is why I prefer to keep a low profile, the least conspicuous of the three founding partners.

"That has to be a record," Leo Foxx says from the doorway. He's our CEO because Checkmate Inc.—a company that started with biologically engineered cologne for men, specifically designed to produce supercharged pheromone responses in women—was born from his doctoral dissertation, but that's another story.

I stop rubbing my eyes and slowly look up.

Dexter Moore appears, also, bracing one shoulder against the doorframe. "I told Leo this one wouldn't last past lunch." Dex is the face of our company with his *GQ* style and tall, dark, and handsome looks. Of the three of us, he ditched the socks and flip-flops look the quickest and easiest, and slid into his role managing our upscale chain of retail studios exclusively for men, which recently expanded into Europe and Dubai.

Leo digs a twenty out of his wallet and places it in Dex's open palm.

"Fuck you both," I grumble.

Dex laughs and stuffs the bill into his shirt pocket. "Fuck you, too, buddy."

If I didn't love my partners like brothers, I'd kick their asses for constantly making me the butt of their jokes.

Never mind that I deserve it for chewing up assistants and spitting them out like gum.

What can I say? I don't like letting new people into my world. I tried that once and got screwed, so I have little room in my circle of influence for new people. Especially new assistants who usually figure out way too much about their bosses. Like the fact that underneath my expensive jeans, custom-cut sport coats, and untucked, designer dress shirts, this particular boss doesn't fit the company image.

I'm only twenty-nine and already broken on the inside. I guess I always will be.

"I told him I didn't want to be disturbed." I lean back in my chair. As the head of R&D, I'm rarely in my office, spending most of my time developing new products in the lab on a lower floor, where Checkmate's other biochemists focus on work and rarely speak. Just the way I like it. "He disturbed me anyway."

"Because you had an important call holding." Leo's assistant, Leticia, pushes through the small space between my two partners and walks to my desk, waving a pink message slip in one hand. In the other hand, she's cradling papers and her infamous iPad—the device from which she rules the universe. "Your assistant was doing his job." I can hear the frustrated eye roll in her voice as she places the message in front of me. She gives the iPad a slight boost. "This is called technology. I send all messages to an electronic folder, but you *never* check it. You're the only intellectual I know who ignores our latest technological advances." She glares at the pink handwritten message on my desk, then pastes on a fake smile that says she's close to the breaking point.

Judging from the soccer mom stories her three kids and husband have shared with us during company family events, I'd have to agree that Leticia's breaking point isn't to be trifled with.

So I try to look contrite. "I'm not ignoring technology." I oscillate my chair back and forth when her pasty smile deepens and her eyes close and open with deliberate movements. It's a little scary. "I'm ignoring people."

She throws a hand in the air and turns to my partners, who are wearing shit-eating grins. "I've got interviews lined up for him this afternoon."

"That fast?" I bark. "I doubt the one I just fired has even left the building. How do you stay five steps ahead of us?"

She cocks her head to one side. "Because I'm Leticia. Do you not know who you're dealing with yet?" She stalks toward the door, no doubt to go conquer another world for us, but stops in front of Leo and Dex. "One of the applicants is the person we tried to hire for him several months back, but she had to decline our offer due to a family crisis."

"Kendall Tate." Dex nods. "She went to high school upstate with Ava. I met her when I went with Ava to her high school reunion."

Ava is Leo's kid sister. We've been helping Leo look out for her since they lost their parents in a car accident several years ago. Ava was still a kid, and Leo was a student at Columbia. She grew into a beautiful woman and a damn good web designer. She partnered with four more smart as hell women to open 5 Muse Designs, which handles our massive website. Apparently, Dex noticed the beautiful woman part when they were working together on our website design awhile back. Now they're engaged, and the wedding is in a few months.

"Since Ms. Tate is a friend of Ava's, I'm giving her another interview. There are several more good résumés here." Leticia taps the papers under the iPad in her hand. "Dex's assistant went on maternity leave last week, and we need another executive level assistant, or we won't be able to handle the workload that's coming our way."

True. I planted the seed to take Checkmate Inc. public several months back, and Leo bought into the idea. Dex eventually wised up and got on board, too. An Initial Public Offering will offset the mounting costs of expanding our company internationally and will make us even wealthier. It's also going to create a shitstorm of work until the initial stock offering proves to be a success and our early investors are satisfied.

Leticia spins on a heel to stare at me, a fist going to her hip like a mom scolding a precocious child. She's been with us since Checkmate's inception. She's also been like a mother to all three of us, which is why I feel like I'm about to be sent to my room without dinner. "Hire one of these applicants. Suck it up and make it work this time, or one of you three is going to die. I don't care which one." She turns to waltz from the room, handing the papers to Leo as she leaves. "But someone's going to get it if you can't find one person in this stack who can tolerate him." She hooks a thumb at me and sashays through the door.

"I guess that settles it." Leo shuffles through the résumés. "We'll conduct the interviews with you."

Silently, I get up, pull on my white lab coat, and spend the rest of the day in the lab, working on our new line. We plan to release the cutting edge products in conjunction with our public stock offering, which should drive up the value. Then I have lunch alone at a deli down the street, after ignoring my partners' text messages to have lunch with them so we can go over the résumés.

When I return to work, I make my way through Checkmate's sleek, modern rotunda that is gleaming with glass and chrome. Once the elevator starts to rise, I press against the glass wall and look over the grand space below, the black and white flooring and giant chess piece sculptures meant to look like a chess game in progress makes me inwardly smile.

It never fails to take my breath away and fill me with pride.

The elevator dings, but when the doors slide open, I don't turn around.

Once our company goes public, this place...our life's work, will no longer be totally ours. Small pieces of it will belong to hundreds or even thousands of faceless people.

Uncertainty surges through me, and I'm frozen in place. What have I done, leading the charge to take our baby public?

The elevator dings again, and the doors start to slide shut.

I turn just as an arm, which is clad in Tom Ford, shoots through the opening. The doors part with a jerk.

"Uh uh," Dex says low enough for only me to hear. "You're not getting away that easily." He reaches around and presses the Open button. "Come on, Mr. Congeniality. The waiting room is full of eager applicants."

I grumble as I step off and charge past the sitting area, which is indeed filled with several professionally dressed people. From my peripheral, a mane of luxurious, brownish-red hair catches my attention. Involuntarily, I glance in that direction.

Something shifts in my chest when a pair of amber eyes look up at me through stylish, black-framed glasses. Her lips are perfectly painted a bright shade of pink and draw my gaze like a magnet.

All three founding partners have gotten enough press coverage to be recognizable to the general public, so as I blow past with Dex on my heels, the other applicants still. But not Pink. Her expression is fearless, and one side of her mouth lifts in a subtle smile that says *I'm smart and confident, and if you don't want me as an employee, someone else will.*

I nearly miss a step because I'm so focused on Pink. *"Fuck's sake,"* I say under my breath, and keep walking.

I swear, one young lady who looks barely out of high school lets out a fearful whimper.

Oh, for the love of God. My reputation, my very presence can't possibly be that unnerving.

As I enter my office, Leo bolts out of his chair with his cell to his ear. "I forgot Chloe has a doctor's appointment in an hour. Today's the sonogram."

Leo married our public relations rep after a whirlwind courtship and got her pregnant on their honeymoon. He knew she was the one soon after they'd met and he just rolled with it.

I'm happy for my friend, so my gloomy mood lifts long enough for me to say, "Go get 'em, pops." I slug him on the arm as he passes. I'll send them a big bouquet of flowers later.

He thrusts a stack of papers, which I can only assume are the résumés, into Dex's chest.

"I hope the poor kid looks like its mother and not its fugly dad." Dex takes a seat on my office sofa and peruses the résumés. "Seriously," he yells at Leo's retreating back. "Don't worry about us. We've got this."

Leo stops. "*Seriously*," he says to Dex, but nods to me. "Hire someone, and don't let him fuck it up. The board is all over me about the three of us keeping our noses clean. No scandals. Not even a parking ticket until after the IPO is done. And even then, we have to be the paragon of professionalism, or the board can push us out, remember?"

Do I ever. It's one of the pitfalls of taking a company public.

I'm tempted to remind my partners that of the three of us, I'm the only one who wasn't involved in the two near misses Checkmate has had in the scandal department. But Leo darts away, so there's no sense.

I start to sink into my leather executive chair, the midday sun blanketing my office since the outer wall is also solid glass. Not even Manhattan's soaring skyline can block out the sunlight on such a clear summer day.

"Uh uh. Sit over here." Dex points to the open space on the opposite end of the sofa. "It's less intimidating than having you behind a desk."

I scrub a hand over my face and move to the sofa with a plop. "Intimidating is a good thing when dealing with employees. Otherwise, you end up with someone like Leticia who bosses *you* around." Dex, Leo, and I all know we'd be screwed without Leticia. She's the one who slays dragons for us with her mother hen tone, pointing finger, and that damn iPad. So, of course, I'm joking. Mostly. "Let's get this over with."

"Best idea I've heard from you in a long time." Dex hands me the résumé on the top of the stack.

Hell, I took Leo's initial dissertation research and built on it, coming up with the lion's share of new product ideas that've made our company successful. "If that were true, we wouldn't have early investors scratching at our door to gobble up Checkmate stock."

Dex scoffs. "They aren't invested yet. We have a board meeting in a few weeks, and they have to be impressed with our long-term trajectory for the company and our business plan, or they won't buy in. Which will cause our stock prices to plummet the minute the initial stock offering goes live. Our company could devalue by half if the initial investors don't snatch up the stock right away."

I stare at my buddy in horror as he blurts out our potential demise like he's talking about the weather. "And people think I'm the dick out of the three of us."

Dex taps the résumés. "Leo and I prioritized these for you starting with the best since you couldn't drag your grumpy ass to our lunch meeting." He knows I'm not much of a people person, and he's definitely familiar with my aversion to new people who might get too close and figure out too much about me. So, I don't make excuses for my absence.

Leticia sticks her head in. "Ready?"

"As I'll ever be," I spit out with as much enthusiasm as I have when going to the dentist.

Dex shoots me a censuring look. "Yes, we're ready. Send in the first interviewee."

When the young woman who whimpered walks in, announces her name as Sarah Williams, and offers us a trembling handshake, I'm both annoyed and relieved that Pink wasn't Dex and Leo's first choice. *Annoyed* because Pink was hot as hell, and the instantaneous pull I experienced made me want to look at her a whole helluva lot more. *Relieved*...well, for the same reasons. Hiring someone I want to eye fuck would be professional suicide.

We sit, and I let Dex do most of the talking. Besides Sarah's shaky voice, incessant leg bouncing, and nervous looks that keep darting my way, we get through most of the interview unscathed until Dex asks a stupid question. "What type of person do you work with best?"

Her eyes flit in my direction. "Um, people who aren't mean. I don't like bullies." It's obvious she's talking about me when she glances in my direction and actually flinches.

Goddammit. I've barely spoken. How the hell can she already think I'm mean? And then have the nerve to say so during an interview? "I am not a bully," I say slowly so I won't lose my shit. Just because I don't have the best people skills on the planet doesn't mean I'm an asshole.

Okay, admittedly, I *can* be an asshole, but I'm not intentionally callous or heartless. Or rude. All of those things are purely unintentional on my part.

Her leg bouncing increases so much I'm sure it could break the sound barrier.

"No one is saying you're mean, Oscar." Dex only uses my full name when he's pissed or warning me not to unleash the flying monkeys. Pun intended, because you can't go through life with a nickname like Oz and not suffer through a few jokes.

"Well..." Her voice wavers, and she wrings her hands, speaking to Dex. "His tone *is* kind of mean."

And they wonder why I prefer to work with Leticia instead of hiring my own assistant. At twenty-nine, I'm not much older than the millennials we're interviewing, but the generation gap is as vast as the Grand Canyon from rim to rim.

I can't help myself. I growl under my breath. "I'm tough."

The applicant starts to get up, looking like she might cry. "Maybe this isn't a good fit. I'm not feeling like this is a safe pla—"

"You're fired," I blurt.

She whimpers again and covers her mouth.

"She hasn't been hired yet," Dex grounds out.

"Then I've just saved us a lot of trouble," I huff. "If she can insult me at the same time she's asking for a job, then she wouldn't last as my assistant."

She flies to the door as though the thought of working for me terrifies her.

Dex gives me a hard stare. "Nice job. Now you're firing them before they even start to work for us?"

Before I can respond, Leticia walks in. "Really?"

"Maybe he should go apologize," Dex says like I'm not in the room. "So we don't get sued."

"Apologize for what?" I'm incensed. "She called *me* names."

"You could apologize for being...you," Dex smarts off.

"You did most of the talking." My teeth are gritting. "I stayed quiet."

"You're even more intimidating when you're silent," Dex says. "You heard what Leo said about the board, right? We have to keep our reputations squeaky clean."

We erupt into a disagreement. I rarely argue with my business partners or Leticia, because I know they've got my back no matter what. Bringing someone new into the fold is the quickest way to push my buttons, though. I guess I have trust issues.

Rightly so, as far as I'm concerned. People can't be trusted most of the time, so I stick to those few who are tried and true.

One of our main phone lines starts to ring, and Pink appears in front of my office. She goes to the assistant's desk and picks up the handset. I can't hear her, but I fall silent, watching her lips form words.

Our argument subsides when Leticia and Dex pipe down to follow my gaze.

Pink fumbles through the desk drawer, retrieving a message pad and pen. Then she jots something onto the notepad.

"That's Kendall Tate," Dex says.

Leticia heads for the door, obviously to find out why Ms. Tate is answering my phone. I have to admit, I'd like to know myself because it's pretty bold.

I fall in line behind Leticia, and so does Dex. We step into the hall just as Ms. Tate says, "I understand your frustration, but I assure you he's not avoiding you."

The person on the other end of the line is talking with such a forceful tone that we can hear him, although the words are jumbled. Somehow, Pink stands her ground with calm composure.

"You're very important to him. I'll see that he gets your message right away and responds as soon as he possibly can." Then she hangs up.

Hell, even *I* believe her, and I don't know who called.

When she turns to us, I'm mesmerized by the way her feminine, powder pink business dress molds to her gorgeous curves. The neckline is conservative and lined with a string of old fashioned pearls, yet she makes them look chic. The dress is sleeveless, and her arms are tanned. The hem flirts just above her knees and reveals calves that aren't overly muscular but still toned.

Just the way I like a woman.

"Your first interviewee blurted this would be the worst place on Earth to work because you're a..." Pink gives me a neutral look, but amusement glitters in her caramel-colored eyes, and she uses her hands to make air quotes. "Because you're a 'meanie' as she ran through the waiting room in tears to catch the elevator, and the other applicants followed her." Ms. Tate hands me the pink message slip, and I can't help but think how the color matches her perfect lips as I anchor my gaze to her mouth. "No one was around to answer the phone, so I figured it wouldn't hurt to help out." She points to the message. "It was your father, by the way. He sounded...upset."

Ms. Tate doesn't seem the least bit rattled that the others left under such questionable circumstances. Or that the apple might not have fallen far from the family tree. Good, because I hate explaining that I'm not a monster. I just don't like people very much. Lots of highly intelligent people don't have interpersonal skills, so sue me.

Which, apparently, the last interviewee just might do because I offended her.

Not Ms. Tate, though. It's so obvious she's not the type to be cowed by anyone, especially not someone like me, who's all bark and no bite.

Suddenly, I start wondering what it would be like to bite the soft spot behind her ear, nibble on her perfectly painted bottom lip, then move lower to find more pink flesh to pull between my teeth.

Fuck me, but I can't hire a girl I'm already fantasizing over.

No idea why, but I don't feel the typical distrust or suspicion when I look at Ms. Tate. No, my mind doesn't go there. It swerves in a completely different direction.

All I can focus on are those pink lips and how much I want to explore them. I want to know her story. I want to know *her*.

Hiring her is definitely out of the question.

So, fuck me all over again when Dex and Leticia both blurt at the same time, "You're hired."

CHAPTER TWO

My dick hasn't stopped twitching for three solid days. Not since Dex and Leticia hired Kendall Tate—AKA Pink—as my new assistant. They also threatened to take out a hit on me if I screw it up.

So, I did what any guy with a decent size set of balls would do. I hid in my lab and buried myself in work. It was either that or ask Pink if I can bury myself in her, which would likely get Checkmate sued, or, at the very least, get my face slapped. Probably both.

The upside is I've put the finishing touches on our new line of products that is sure to make our stock offering soar once we start the prelaunch advertising campaign. The downside is I'll need to have my new assistant at my side constantly as I ensure the packaging and promotions match the product. It's what I do. I don't just develop the products then hand them off without oversight. I walk my babies through each step until they're ready to ship.

My business partners call my attention to detail obsessive.

I call it quality control and remind them that my obsessiveness is a big part of our success.

Which is why I'm at the office extra early on a Thursday morning, long before anyone else. I'm studying the packaging mock-ups sent up from the Product Management Department.

I've got photos of the prototypes laid out on my desk as I sip coffee that I picked up at my favorite coffee shop on the corner. They get up at the ass crack of dawn just like me and start making my order the second I open the door without me having to ask. I like it strong and black.

As a joke between friends, Dex and Leo often tell me my choice of coffee matches my usual mood.

I often call them assholes. And I'm only partially joking.

I take another drink from the to-go cup, letting the robust flavor roll over my taste buds. Not even the extraordinary flavor and jolt of caffeine can keep me focused.

I open my desk drawer and withdraw Kendall's personnel file so I can find out more about her. She's twenty-six and overqualified for this job. In just a few years, she worked her way up at an event planning company in the city, orchestrating everything from small wedding brunches to large, citywide events for thousands of people, until the company laid her off due to financial problems.

Why would she settle for an assistant's position that's a huge step down the ladder of success?

The waiting room lights flicker on, and just as she rounds the corner, I pull my attention away from reviewing Kendall's work experience. She's holding two cups of coffee in a drink carrier, and a light pink leather purse is hooked into the crease of her elbow.

She waves and boosts the coffees, indicating one is likely for me.

Without thinking, I toss my cup into the trash beneath my desk so as not to disappoint her. She went to the trouble of bringing coffee. The least I can do is show some appreciation.

Goddammit.

I do not need to show appreciation for a damn cup of coffee. Or for the fact that she's here, ready and eager to work before anyone else.

Or for the fact that she's dressed to kill, just like she's been every damn day since we hired her.

I shove her file in the desk drawer and slam it shut as she

discards the purse onto her desk and comes to stand in my doorway.

"Morning, boss." Her stilettos match the color of her purse. She's wearing a taupe, polka-dotted dress that fits her like a glove, and my eyes are drawn to the thin, light pink belt that matches her other accessories and forms a small bow right about where her belly button should be.

I can't help it. I just fucking can't. I lick my lips.

"Morning." To my surprise, I manage to sound normal, as though I'm completely unaware that she's a knockout.

She nods to the drink carrier. "I brought an extra. It's yours if you want it."

Oh, I want it. Unfortunately, I can't have it. And I'm not talking about the coffee.

"I could use some caffeine," I lie like a damn *dog*. Hopefully, she won't see the half-full cup in the trash.

She walks over and sets the carrier on my desk, retrieving her cup and leaving the other for me, along with packets of sugar and cream. "I brought all the *fixins*." She stresses the last word with a playful smile and a manufactured southern drawl.

I've done the same thing since I went to a swanky summer camp for rich kids in North Carolina when I was twelve. It irritates my parents, because any twang other than a Hyannis Port-Kennedy accent sounds low class to them. God forbid anyone think we're middle class or even close. To them, a southern drawl sounds unintelligent and uneducated, which is why I still do it.

Kendall's fake accent is cute as hell.

I almost bite my tongue just for thinking the word *cute*.

She takes a step back from my desk and cradles her cup with both hands.

I hold my breath, hoping she'll wrap those lush lips, which are painted that exquisite color of pink once again, around the spout of her cup for a sip. Or a long, slow pull. Either would work for me, but I gotta be honest and say I'm rooting for the long, slow pull.

"I left it black, though, since I don't know how you like it."

The swell in my pants grows larger. That's saying something since I'm pretty well hung. I'd love to show her how I like it. Even better, I'd love for her to show me how *she* likes it.

To calm my racing pulse, I grab the fresh cup of brew. "It's perfect, thanks." I shove the cup to my mouth and gulp down more liquid gold.

And then the most extraordinary thing happens. This woman, who has occupied my every waking moment since I first laid eyes on her and has even taken up residence in my dirty dreams but hasn't shown an ounce of interest in me beyond her responsibilities as my assistant, lets her gaze wander to my mouth. It stays there, a small part forming between her plump pink lips.

I still, the cup hovering at chin level. The office is silent since we're alone, but I swear I hear the snap, crackle, pop of an electrical current in the air shifting and swirling around us.

"Pink," I half-whisper. No idea how the hell I let that slip.

Her brow crinkles, and her unusual amber eyes snap up to meet mine. "Excuse me?"

Fuck. There's a line here that I can't cross. Crossing it could create a scandal, and a scandal is the last thing Checkmate needs right before our stock offering goes public.

"I...I..." I stutter like an idiot, scrambling to cover my mistake. "Your matching pink..." *Your matching pink fuck me heels that I'd love to feel biting into my ass and pink belt that sits right where I'd like to put my tongue...* I pull my mind out of the gutter. Okay, it's only halfway out of the gutter, but I'll take it because I'm fighting so damn hard to stay calm, cool, and semi-collected. "Your matching pink stuff gave me an idea."

I lean forward and tap the photos on my desk. "These are the mock-ups for our new product line that's launching soon." I spread them out more as she walks around to my side of the desk to take a look. When her sexy sweet scent of tropical flowers and ocean water rolls over me like a warm summer breeze, I scoot my chair farther away to put space between us.

Her intoxicating perfume having the very effect on me that our products are meant to have on women isn't lost on me.

I refocus on the mock-ups. The bottles of men's cologne and personal hygiene products are so obviously meant to appeal to men. They're jet black and shaped into a stallion's head, the silver artwork on the front making the horse's mane seem like it's in motion, just like our company logo. "What if we added subtle pink highlights to the artwork?"

Huh. Not a bad idea considering I just pulled that out of my ass as a cover.

Kendall studies the photos. "You think pink will appeal to men?"

I so fucking do. My gaze drops to her painted lips.

"Do *you* think it will?" I find myself asking because her opinion matters to me far more than it should.

She angles her body toward me, propping a hip against my desk. "I think a man who's confident in himself and isn't afraid to take a risk will be intrigued by the color. It's bold and interesting. Just taboo enough to make a man want it, mainly because he knows he shouldn't."

Holy shit. Is she saying what I think she's saying?

Or is it just wishful thinking on my dirty-minded part?

Either way, not gonna happen. Not unless I add her to the long list of former assistants who I've fired.

CHAPTER THREE

Product Management puts a rush on the color changes I want for our new product line, the prototypes are done, and the Manufacturing Department has taken over, so the initial shipments will be ready to roll out by the time Checkmate stock goes live on the New York Stock Exchange.

Which means the shitstorm of work has hit us in full force.

We've got under two weeks to put together a kick-ass presentation for our board, which comprises the bulk of our initial investors. The presentation has to have a wow factor that will knock the board members' fifteen-hundred-dollar *Harry's of London* socks off.

Seriously, anyone who's willing to pay that kind of cash for a pair of damn socks is going to be hard to please. I should know. My dad owns several pairs.

Thank fuck he's not one of our investors. If he was, we'd be screwed, which is why I purposefully haven't returned Dad's call. Or the half dozen or so additional messages he's yelled into Kendall's ear. I've apologized to her for each one.

I'm not close to my father, so not calling him back right away shouldn't be a surprise to him. No idea why he's being such an ass about it to my assistant, other than the fact that he's...well, an ass. It'll be a while before I return his messages, because I don't want to give Dad a chance to ask questions about work. We've kept the IPO under wraps, even having our employees sign a nondisclosure statement to keep our secret. But Dad's an ace at sniffing out solid investments. Hence, his fondness for overpriced socks and his ability to pay for them.

Everyone on the executive floor has been working almost twenty-four-seven. I look up from the spreadsheets, flow charts, and prototypes that are spread across the table in the conference room and push my chair back to rub my bleary eyes. It's not quite noon, and we've already put in the equivalent of a full workday. Pink is sitting across from me and is engrossed in the PowerPoint presentation I've asked her to create.

Pink's hair has a chic, weekend tousled look, pulled back into a ponytail with lots of messy tendrils falling around her face and shoulders. She's so intent on her work that her glasses have slipped down her nose, and she's nibbling on one side of her bottom lip. Since it's Saturday, she's wearing a plain white ladies' tee with a front pocket. The sleeves are rolled up almost to shoulder level. She's sporting that trendy, half-tucked look, where the shirt is inserted into the front of her baggy boyfriend jeans but hanging free everywhere else.

To keep from staring at her, I look at the floor, my gaze snagging on her legs and feet under the table. Her jeans are cuffed at the ankles, revealing a pair of beaded sandals that show off slender, feminine feet and toenails painted a shade of neon pink that belongs on a beach in the Caribbean.

Goddammit, now I'm picturing her in a bikini with bright sunshine shimmering off her soft, supple skin. Skin that's beaded with moisture so that it's slick.

Yes, definitely wet and slick.

Without looking up from her work, she readjusts in her chair, and her toes wiggle.

My mouth waters because I want to put my lips around her perfectly painted pinky toe and suck.

No, I don't have a damned foot fetish. Or at least I didn't until now.

Shit. I exhale hard.

Her head snaps up. "Everything okay?"

No, everything is not fucking okay. "It's great."

I pinch the bridge of my nose. "Just a little brain dead. Some lunch and a strong cup of coffee and I'll be good as new."

With a dainty nudge, she pushes her glasses up the bridge of her nose and levels a concerned look at me. "I'll go get us lunch. What are you in the mood for?" I swear her voice turns smoky and seductive.

So I don't blurt *you,* I bite the inside of my cheek. It hurts like a motherfucker.

The sensual banter, the sexual chemistry she and I have been circling—because I know a thing or two, or forty thousand, about chemistry and can no longer ignore it—has to end.

"I've got a better idea." I push out of my chair. "I'll get food orders for the rest of the crew, and we'll both go get lunch. I need a break from this place." So I can tell her I'd like to help her find a job with another company so I can date her. If she's game. And unless I'm the stupidest smart guy in the Big Apple, her signals are telling me she's definitely game. "The walk to the deli down the street might do me some good." So would getting laid, but there's zero chance of that for the foreseeable future because of working around the clock to prepare for the board meeting. And because the only person I want to help me out with that particular project is currently my assistant.

"I'll get the orders," she says. "I'm the assistant, remember?"

Yes, I fucking remember. It's the very problem I'm trying to solve.

Grabbing a pad and pen, she heads for the door, leaving me standing there with nothing to do but scratch my balls. Metaphorically, of course.

See, this is the problem with my new, over-qualified assistant. She runs circles around me. She's the only assistant I've had who seems to naturally know how to handle my abrasive personality. In fact, I'm not my normal, caustic self around her, which is weird as hell. She's also the only assistant I've ever wanted to keep.

Therein lies the problem.

I want to keep my assistant and I want to eat her, too.

She disappears through the conference room door, the round cheeks of her ass filling out those boyfriend jeans a little more than they should. You'd think the loose fitting pants would shift my imagination into park and my dick into neutral.

But *naw*. Both are still in overdrive.

Ten minutes later we're riding down the elevator.

Thank God I wear my shirts untucked.

When we push through the glass doors of Checkmate HQ and step out onto the sidewalk, Manhattan's weekend crowd hustles and flows around us. I look up at the blue sky, letting the warmth of the bright sun soak through me while Pink pulls an eyeglass case from her purse and switches into a pair of mirrored sunglasses.

Of course, the reflective coating is tinted pink.

"C'mon." I don't know what possesses me, but I place my hand on her elbow and lead her to the curb, where I hail a cab.

"Where are we going?" The tenor of her voice is a little frantic as I open the door and she gets in, sliding over to make room for me.

"Anywhere but here." I close the cab door. "West 27th." I give the cabbie the address to one of my favorite restaurants in the city. It's unique without all the pomp and circumstance I grew up with, which is one of the reasons I like it. It's a public place for private affairs, and like it or not, I need to discuss the future of her employment with Checkmate, or lack thereof. If she's interested in taking our relationship to a personal level, I'll make some calls to help her find gainful employment outside of Checkmate Inc.

I'll hire another assistant immediately and move heaven and

earth to make it work this time. Of course, I'll have to wear protective armor to keep Leticia from killing me with the poisoned darts that will surely shoot from her eyes, but a chance to get to know Pink intimately is well worth it. She's the only woman who has piqued my interest in a long, long time. First, I just have to discuss her termination and employment elsewhere.

So that we can hopefully get naked together.

My brain stutters.

No, I didn't lie about my IQ. I'm just now hearing in my own head that I'm hoping she'll go out with me *after* I fire her, and I'm fully aware that it sounds as moronic to me as it's going to sound to my partners. But not nearly as moronic as it would sound to our Legal Department if Pink and I can't stem the tide of attraction that is barreling toward us.

I hold out my hand. "Gimme the lunch orders."

The creases above her sunglasses deepen, but she digs around in her purse and pulls out...*an unopened package of Krazy Glue?*

"Nope." She tosses it on the seat between us and dives in again. Next, she retrieves an egg-shaped container of Silly Putty.

By the time she frees a Tide to-go pen, a keto snack bar, a package of Disney princess Band-Aids, and a bobble head of the Queen of England, I can't help but say something. "Good Lord, woman. You might as well carry around a portable storage unit."

For the first time since I met her, that air of confidence she wears so well disappears. I want to kick my own ass because I want Confident Pink back. At the same time, it's oddly comforting to know she's not as perfect as she seems. The purse thing is exasperating, so I'll build on that and look for more flaws to keep my mind off wanting her if she shoots down what I'm about to propose.

"Sorry." The quiver of her chin is barely noticeable when she lifts the corner of her mouth ever so slightly, revealing a tiny dimple.

Okay, the kissable dimple trumps the annoying purse. I want her more than ever now.

"Carrying a lot in my bag has become a habit."

Obviously.

"I..." She stills as though she's not sure how much to share. "Never mind."

Curiosity twitches in my brain like the whiskers on a cat. I smell a story. A story that will pull at my heartstrings, I'm sure of it...and my gut instincts are rarely wrong. I'm my father's son, after all.

It's the reason I was willing to take a risk on a crazy idea that turned into Checkmate Inc. It's the reason I knew I should bail on my first engagement, even as bridezilla walked down the aisle toward me. Too bad I didn't listen that time. Mainly because I was afraid my father would use a cattle prod to get me back to the altar if I tried to bolt.

The purse searching, which seems to be an effort to dig all the way to China, resumes, and Pink pulls a notepad free. "Here it is."

I've got the corner deli's app out and the orders typed in before she's returned all the items to her purse. I pay the extra charge for the deli to deliver the food to Checkmate's executive floor and put my phone on silent just as Pink stuffs the bobble head into the bag. A gloved waving hand protrudes through the opening, mocking me for wanting to know why she's carrying it around.

So, I gotta ask. "What's with Queen Elizabeth?"

Pink laughs softly. "It's my niece's. I...um...I was watching her a lot before I moved back to the city." And there it goes again. That miniscule waver in her confidence. A crack in her armor. It's back, and I don't like it. Not one damn bit. "I took her to the park recently and she asked me to hold it while she played on the swings. I forgot to give it back."

When we pull up in front of the Oscar Wilde restaurant, Pink climbs out of the cab, her expression awestruck.

My chest inflates because I've obviously made her happy.

"I've heard about this place." Her voice is as astonished as the look on her face. "When it was about to open, it was all the rage in the world of event planning. I never got the chance to check it out before I lost my job." She shrugs sarcastically. "Then I was broke and couldn't afford to eat out. And had to move back in with my folks upstate." She gives me a playful wink. "But things are looking up. I'm making bank at my new job. My boss is adventurous and takes me along with him to interesting places when he needs a break."

Her gaze flits over the storefront, taking in the Victorian fleur-de-lis stenciling that borders the massive windows. A bronze, life-sized statue of Oscar himself sits on a park bench in front of the restaurant. "Do you know it houses the longest bar in the city?"

I nod, enjoying her enthusiasm. "I do know that."

"It's fascinating," she says.

And the reason I love the place myself.

"It was the Prohibition Enforcement Headquarters back in the day, which is wonderfully ironic, don't you think?" She positively glows.

"Now *that* I didn't know." I'm impressed that she's schooling me. It's a nice change. Fresh. Exciting. Sexy as all hell.

"I would've loved to plan an event here." Her voice goes wistful and I hear traces of disappointment.

I take her elbow again and start to lead her to the door. I've got her on a subject of which I'd like to further explore: herself, her past, and why she's working for me.

"Wait!" She steps up to the statue. "Come on." She waves me over, pulling out her phone. "I want a selfie with the two Oscars." She snorts with laughter.

It's so damn cute I play along.

There isn't enough room on the bench for both of us, so she points to the empty spot next to the metal Oscar Wilde. "Sit. I'll kneel in front of you."

Jesus fucking Christ.

I sit just as three ladies in their mid-forties walk out of the restaurant. Their volume is dialed up, telling me they've had a few too many of the exotic drinks offered at the restaurant's whisky bar.

"Awwww." The lady in front stops, the other two bumping into

her. "What a lovely couple." She looks from me to Pink. The other two coo in agreement. "Let's take your picture." She snatches Pink's phone and steps back. "Go on, sit on his lap."

Oh, hell no. If she sits on my lap, my overactive imagination will be outed. "I'm not sure—"

Pink slides onto my lap, adjusting to get comfortable. Wiggling her ass against my thighs and crotch to find the right pose for the picture.

I know the second she realizes I want her. Her eyes fly wide and snap to mine, a tiny gasp slipping through her plump pink lips.

Dammit, I'm an asshole.

Our gazes lock, and time stops. Her soft breaths feather over my cheek, and I bite back a groan.

"What an adorable shot," the drunk lady says. She's obviously been snapping pictures of the whole scene. "Now lay one on him, girlfriend, because by the look on his face, he'd rather have you for lunch than anything on Oscar's menu."

They have no idea.

The happy hour threesome erupts into giggles. "Go ahead. I'm not giving back the phone until you kiss."

This is worse than getting caught on a kiss cam at a Knicks game. You just know it's going to be all over social media before the game is over and you'll catch hell from every dude you know.

In this case, I'm likely to catch hell from my partners and my investors if I'm caught on camera, making out with my new assistant.

So why the hell do I find myself placing my open palm against the back of Pink's head? Her silky hair is so soft against my rough hand as I reach up with my other hand to cup her cheek and angle her mouth to fit perfectly against mine.

The kiss is slow. Soft. Sweet.

More oooohs and aaaaahs come from the three tipsy ladies who are taking our picture, but I don't stop. How can I? Pink's amazing lips part just enough for my tongue to slip through and graze over hers.

A sensual sound escapes from the back of Pink's throat. It's low enough so that only I can hear it.

I break the kiss, but not because I want to. No, Pink stares down at me, and it's obvious that we both know we're thoroughly screwed.

CHAPTER FOUR

Oscar Wilde's is bustling. I slip the hostess a Ben Franklin and have her seat Pink and me in a quiet corner. I need at least a little privacy when I pitch my idea to terminate her employment, so I can then ask her out on a date.

I know, I know. I'm a dumbass. But the right woman can do that to a guy, and Pink is the first girl I've met since my divorce who I feel in my gut is worth the risk.

As we follow the hostess to the back corner, Pink's posture is rigid. The wonderful curiosity this place evokes in its patrons is lost on both of us after the incredible kiss we just shared. Obviously, Pink isn't sure what to make of it or what to do about it.

But I do. All I need is the right opening, and I'll explain my plan for us to get what I'm hoping we both want, each other.

The hostess places menus in front of us. "This is called our Temptation Room."

Of course it is. I shake my head at the ridiculousness of the situation as the hostess draws the Victorian drapes, leaving us in the small, quaint chamber.

As soon as we're alone, Pink changes from sunglasses to regular glasses, flips open her menu, and studies it like a textbook. The small bistro table starts to shake as she obviously bounces her leg with nervous energy.

Is she scared of me the way the interviewee was? It makes me bristle that Pink might think I'm a mean bully. Yet another clue that she's special because I don't usually care what people think.

I draw in a deep breath and let my gaze coast over her. When her intense expression stays trained on the menu, I reach under the table and place a hand on her bouncing knee. Not smart, I know. Touching her like this is dangerous, but it seems right.

So fucking right.

Her leg stills against my touch, and she looks up at me. I don't like what I see there.

"Don't be afraid of me," I say. "I'd never pressure you for anything." I hold her gaze. "Hell, it's the opposite." I lift my chin toward the door. "What happened out there can't happen again as long as you're working for me. Checkmate has too much at stake."

"Then get your hand off my thigh," she fires at me.

I sit back, folding my arms in front of me. "I'm sorry. I guess I misread your signals. You didn't seem to mind when I shoved my tongue down your throat, so forgive me for getting confused. You have my word it won't happen again."

She lets her gaze drop to the menu again, but her eyes are darting over it so fast I know she's only pretending to read. "You didn't misread the signals," she whispers. "I just..." Her voice wavers as she weighs her words. "I'm incredibly attracted to you, and I know it's stupid to put myself in that position with my boss."

Not only does my dick roar to life, but my ego soars as blood pounds through my veins.

Pink wants me as much as I want her. The fact that she's bold and confident enough to say so is such a damn turn on.

Plus, she just mentioned putting herself in a position with me. I've got about a dozen or so in mind. All we have to do is wait until she's working elsewhere, and we can try any of them. I'll let her pick, gentleman that I am.

"I'm sorry," she says.

"Don't apologize for making my fucking day."

Her mesmerizing amber eyes lift from the menu and hook into mine. Only the small tremble in her fingers as she does that dainty little maneuver that pushes her glasses farther up the bridge of her nose gives away the sexual tension that's obviously coursing through her.

She shakes her head. "I agree, it can't happen again. I need this job. Badly." The desperation in her tone matches the look in her pretty eyes. "I can't afford to screw it up."

Now we're getting somewhere.

The server moves the curtain aside and steps into the Temptation Room. Without breaking eye contact with Pink, I hold up a finger. "Give us a minute." The server scurries away because my tone is so brash. "Why do you need this job so much?" When she hesitates, I say, "Please, tell me." My gruff tone is gone, replaced by softness that surprises me as much as it obviously does her.

Her lips part, and I want to kiss her again. Not soft this time, but hard and demanding until she's begging me for more. Begging me to undress her. Begging me to fuck her.

"Pink," I whisper, my gaze anchoring to her lips.

"What?" Her brow furrows.

I'm so busted, and I can't bring myself to lie.

I look away, a little embarrassed. "It seems like the perfect nickname." I can't help but focus on her lips. "You wear so much of it." My voice turns husky. "It looks so fucking amazing on you, especially on your lips."

Her big eyes round into saucers, and she swallows.

God Almighty, *she swallows.*

I lace my fingers on top of the table. "Look, we're both in the same rocking boat. We obviously..." *Want to rip our clothes off and lick every square inch of each other.* I scrub a hand over my scruffy jaw. It's Saturday, after all, and I didn't bother to shave. "We obviously—"

"Want to go to a hotel instead of back to the office?" She says it as though it's the only obvious way to finish my sentence.

I nearly swallow my tongue.

"Excellent idea that it is, we can't do that while you're employed at Checkmate." I lean forward, and the bistro table is so small that I'm close enough for her subtly sweet scent to prickle my senses. "Kendall, I have a solution for our...uh, problem...but first, I need to ask a few questions."

The table starts to shake again.

"Stop bouncing your leg. I told you there's no reason to be afraid of me, and I meant it," I say. "You can trust me."

She gives her head a shake and blows out a laugh. "I don't know why, but I believe you."

"Then tell me why you need this job so badly, and why did you take a job so far beneath your skill set to begin with?"

She rubs the back of her neck. "Can we order first? Maybe even have a glass of wine? I know we're working, but we've already crossed a few professional boundaries today, and I could stand to loosen up a little."

"It's Saturday, so it's not technically office hours." I go to the drape and wave over the waitress. Pink and I both ask for today's special. It's easier than pondering the menu choices.

Pink orders a French Cab by the glass.

Fuck it.

I tell the waitress to bring the whole bottle. Something tells me we're going to need it, and we can make up for the extended lunch break by working longer tomorrow.

Once Pink has one glass of wine down, I pour her another. "Okay, I'm listening."

She holds the wine at chest level, tapping an elegant, manicured nail against the glass. "The short version is I need the money to help my younger sister maintain custody of her daughter."

Okay. Obviously, there are a few blanks that need filling in, but I'm guessing Pink is talking about the niece she mentioned in the taxi. "Would your sister's daughter happen to be the owner of a bobble head queen?"

"One and the same." Pink chuckles.

The sound of her bubbly laughter eases the tension between

my shoulder blades. Unfortunately, it does nothing for the tension going on beneath my zipper. "And the long version of the story would be?"

She sets down her glass, growing serious. Suddenly, Pink is animated with fire in both her tone and her eyes. "My niece's father is wealthy." Pink peers over her eyeglasses for dramatic effect. "I mean *really* wealthy."

This doesn't faze me like it obviously does her. I grew up with a silver spoon in my mouth big enough to feed the Statue of Liberty. "And?"

"*And* when my sister got pregnant, he wouldn't marry her." Pink looks both sad and pissed at the same time. "His family didn't approve."

Ah, so we're talking about *that* kind of money. Sounds familiar. "You may not believe this, but your sister is probably better off." I should know. I've chosen to live in a different world than my family. I left behind the privileged, upper-crust crowd the second I found my ex banging every man in her path before our first anniversary, then she couldn't understand why I wanted out because of how it would look at my mom and dad's house parties in the Hamptons—and my parents actually agreed with her.

Pink knocks back more wine, and then nods. "Probably. She's better off in every way except financially."

"That rich fucker doesn't pay child support?" I blurt, acid climbing up my throat to leave a bitter taste in my mouth.

"Not a dime. Never has, and his family never acknowledged my niece." Pink gives me a resigned stare. "Until now."

How can someone abandon their own kid? Jesus, I thought my folks were bad.

Then again, money often turns people into selfish assholes without them realizing it. My mother is my father's third country-club wife. I have an older half-brother named Grant, who wields that giant silver spoon I mentioned like a weapon, as though it gives him the right to lie, cheat, and act a cut above regular, hard-working folks.

That's why I never touch my trust fund. That's also why I don't use my family name—Randolph. Strong is my grandmother's maiden name. I started using it in college so I could make my own way in the world, not wanting anyone to know I was a trust fund baby.

I haven't done too badly, if I do say so myself.

I made the name change legal after my divorce. I'd played the good son as best I could, trusting Dad's judgment and following his advice. Even marrying the woman of his choice fresh out of college, only to be crushed by her lying eyes and cheating ways within months.

Now that I think of it, Mom and Dad should've fixed up Grant with my ex. They would've been a perfect match, and definitely would've deserved each other.

It's the reason I never go around him. The reason I refuse to be like him, and instead aspire to be like the *working-class peasants* Grant disdains.

"What part of the equation changed for them to want to acknowledge her now?" I ask.

Pink gives me an appreciative smile. "I love it that your mind stays a step ahead."

Not really. My mind's been four steps behind and wallowing in the gutter since the second I laid eyes on Pink. "I'm pretty good at equations and identifying unknown factors."

She smiles, but then it disappears, and wetness shimmers in her eyes.

I swear I have to stop *my* leg from bouncing. I don't know why, but my protective instincts are already on alert. I'm ready to go to war for Pink, and I don't even know her story yet. "What? Tell me."

"My niece is losing her hearing and needs cochlear implants. My sister's a waitress." Pink doesn't offer a broader explanation. Doesn't have to.

Waitresses don't usually have insurance coverage, and they sure as hell don't make enough money to cover a major health problem.

"I'm so sorry." I reach across the table and cover Pink's hand with mine. Displays of affection aren't my thing, but when she doesn't pull away, my heart thumps and bumps against my chest. I caress a finger across the back of her hand. "How does this affect custody of your niece?"

"My sister was desperate and went to her daughter's grandparents for help." She rolls her eyes. "Loving grandparents that they obviously are, they agreed to pay for everything my niece needs, under one condition..." The fire is back, and Pink sits forward. "Those assholes, who've never even met their own granddaughter, want full custody." She huffs with exasperation. "So she'll have the *right upbringing.*"

Pink is right. Baby Daddy and his parents are assholes of the highest order. And Pink obviously took a job that's beneath her to help her sister.

"I'm guessing it's all or nothing with them? They won't help with the cost at all unless your sister gives up her daughter to them."

"You got it." Pink shakes her head with disgust. "I seriously don't know what's wrong with people like that. It's turned me off of old money people for good. I want nothing to do with people who are born into privilege."

I get it. Obviously, I do, but a blanket statement like that is a bit harsh. I'm nothing like my family, and I'm certainly not like her niece's grandparents, who are essentially splashing their money around to buy a kid from its mother.

That's beyond fucked up.

I don't want Pink to think less of me, though, so I don't tell her about my family's wealth. "Why didn't you hold out for a job in your field instead of working as an executive assistant? It has to be a step down for you."

"I was trying to, but no one offered the same salary I'd been making. The higher paying jobs are going to people with more experience than me. Honestly, I'm good at my job, but I've only been out of college four years." She shrugs. "Couldn't afford rent here in the city without a job, so I moved back upstate to live with my folks while I was job hunting." She stares at my fingers moving over hers. "I've never been one to sit around. I worked three jobs to put myself through college, so I got a job at the diner my sister's been working for since she graduated high school and kept sending out résumés. I figured it was a good way to stay busy. That's where I met your partner, Dex. The first time I called for an interview, Leticia literally hired me over the phone."

Pink snags her ponytail with one hand and fingers the silky strands. "But then my niece was diagnosed, and I decided to stay upstate because my family needed me. My parents and I took turns babysitting so my sister could pick up extra shifts at the diner." She twists her hair around an index finger. "But the proce-dure my niece needs can cost tens of thousands of dollars." Pink's chin quivers. "Maybe more. And her hearing is deteriorating so fast that there is no way my sister can save the money quick enough."

"And that's when you called us for another interview...so you can help out your sister." It's not a question because I'm sure I'm right.

Pink nods. "Thank you for paying so well. I'm making more money as your assistant than any of the event jobs I've been offered since I was laid off. I send my sister as much money as I can every month. We have to save enough for the down payment, then we can have the procedure done and make monthly payments on the balance."

"I'll give you the money," I blurt, squeezing Pink's hand as though that will wring the sadness out of her. I don't tell her that I grew up in the same world as her niece's grandparents because I don't want to lose this thing that's happening between us.

Her expression blanks. "No," she finally says, extricating her hand from mine. "I wouldn't feel right about it."

Smart girl. She doesn't know me well enough to be beholden to me, especially since she's my assistant. "Okay, then call it a loan. We can draw up a contract so there's no strings." *Then I can help you find another job. A better job that pays more.* With my connections, all it will take is a few calls. And then we can move on. See where this thing between us might lead.

I'm hoping it leads to candlelight dinners, walks in Central Park, long nights of incredible sex, but I guess I'm getting ahead of myself. First, I need to convince Pink that she should take my offer, then we can target companies for potential employment. I can call in a few favors, and *bang*.

Yep, bang. As in me and Pink going at it until we're sweaty and spent. Neither of us having to worry about an inappropriate office romance.

"*No,*" Pink says as the server delivers our food. "My parents aren't flashy. They're just hardworking people who taught me to earn my own way." She forks up a bite. "My family takes care of its own. What I need more than anything right now is stability, and that's what I have at Checkmate Inc. The job as your assistant is the solution to my niece's problem, so it's going to be my primary focus. I promise to do a superior job and earn everything you're paying me, plus some."

Selfish, I know, but I have to ask. "How long will it take you to save up the money for your niece's procedure?" What I'm really wanting to know is how long before she can leave Checkmate, so I can ask her out.

"First the down payment, then paying off the procedure." She lifts a shoulder. "I'm guessing a long time."

I don't say anything as my stomach drops to my feet.

She takes another bite and washes it down with a gulp of wine. "Okay, your turn." She's holding the wine glass to her lips but lifts her index finger to waggle it between her and me. "You said you have a solution to our...problem." She shoots me a dazzling smile that's laced with just enough naughtiness to make the blood pumping through my thudding heart rush to my prick.

I stab at my food, unable to completely hide my disappointment, and I shake my head. "Never mind. It's a bad idea." It wasn't just bad, it was impulsive as hell because I was thinking with my dick and not my brain.

There are times when a high IQ and multiple science degrees are worthless. This seems to be one of them.

"Let's focus on the IPO. When it's a success, Checkmate will hand out employee raises and bonuses like cologne samples at our retail studios." I give Pink a half-hearted smile. "That will ultimately help your niece, and she's most important right now."

Pink gives me a small smile, her eyes turning so smoky that I can see she wants me even more now that she's glimpsed my softer side. Not something I often show to people, especially if they're not a member of my trusted inner circle. "Thank you." Disappointment threads through her whispered words.

I know exactly how she feels.

"You're welcome." How can I say anything else? No way am I going to put my selfish desires ahead of a little girl who's going deaf. I might be a gruff asshole sometimes, but I'm not a complete douche.

So why do I feel like such a dick for secretly wanting the little girl's father to man up and own up to his responsibilities without strings attached? For wanting Pink to move on to a different job? For not caring how much Checkmate needs Pink's skills right now?

All so I can have her in my bed.

Yes, Dick should be my middle name.

CHAPTER FIVE

At the office, I've become the poster child for the #metoo movement. A paragon of professionalism that will make our investors slash board members happy. Respectful treatment of women is something I stand behind and the very thing that planted the seed which became Checkmate Inc. to begin with. But it doesn't make me want my new assistant any less. I just have to keep my desires, not to mention my filthy imagination, to myself.

Never mind that I've got more tension in my shoulders than a rope during a tug-of-war game.

It's been a week since I took Pink...excuse me...since I took *Kendall* to Oscar Wilde's restaurant.

See? Professional.

Yes, it's been a full seven days since I discovered how selfish my idea was to help Kendall find another job so we could date. A week since I realized how ridiculous it would be to let go of the best damned assistant I've ever had just because I want to give her so many orgasms she'd lose count.

Actually, it's been six days, five hours, and forty-seven minutes. Not that I'm counting.

I run fingers through my hair and glance at the clock on my office wall, the *ticktock, ticktock* mocking me.

Kendall appears in the doorway. "Ready?"

Just the sight of her makes heat skate over my skin.

Yes, I'm ready to do a dry run of my presentation to make sure it's perfect before our board meeting next week. I don't say that, though. My gaze slides over her, and I bite back a groan. The enormous amount of restraint I'm exercising is agonizing.

"So ready." My voice is all gravel and gloom.

Swear to God, her eyes turn to smoke and fire.

But we can't do anything to satisfy the pull of lust we so obviously feel, and we both know it. Hence, the gloomy tone.

Kendall clears her throat, as though she's trying to stay focused. "I've got the PowerPoint presentation set up in the conference room. Leticia is rounding up Dex and Leo, and Gerard and Magnus are on their way up, too."

When Dex came up with the idea to expand Checkmate Inc. into a chain of upscale retail studios, he had the foresight to snag Magnus and his husband, Gerard, away from the fashion scene in Milan. Now they oversee our foreign studios that have been opening throughout Europe and Dubai. We flew them in for the board meeting because they're an integral part of our success. I mean, come on. Three straight geeks like me, Leo, and Dex? We were in over our heads before the words *retail studios for men* even left Dex's mouth.

Kendall slides back the cuff of her dusty pink wraparound blazer, which stylishly flows over the waist of a pair of white pants that hit her just above very nice ankles, and glances at her Apple watch. "We're on in five." She hurries away.

I stand and adjust the waistband of my jeans. I wish I could say the hard wood in my pants was just standard morning glory, but it's almost quitting time on a Friday afternoon. No morning glory to it. Just plain old unrequited lust from working closely with a woman I can't get out of my mind.

I take a moment to think of my ex-wife. Of the betrayal. Of the heartache.

And yup. My arousal disappears, and I get my game face on.

Much, much less uncomfortable than getting a hard-on when I'm about to walk into a room full of my closest friends and colleagues.

When I stroll into the conference room, everyone is seated around the long table. Leticia is pouring a glass of fruit-infused water for Dex, then moves around the table doing the same for each person. Kendall is at the far end, with an open laptop and an empty chair for me, where she set up mission control for the mock presentation.

Leo is shoving his phone in Magnus and Gerard's face, and they're gasping and fanning their eyes over the sonogram pictures of Leo and Chloe's unborn baby.

Magnus—who was my personal life-stylist before we moved him overseas—starts to *tsk* the second he sees me. "Oscar, *daaaaling.*"

Gerard looks up from the in utero baby pictures and starts shaking his head in unison with Magnus's *tsking*. No wonder they make such a perfect couple. "What have they done to you, *mon amie?*" Living in Europe has all but erased Gerard's West Virginia drawl.

"I *must* have a chat with your new life-stylist." Magnus actually leans forward to look at my shoes, and the lines of disapproval creasing the space between his perfectly waxed brows deepens.

"You mean a disciplinary meeting," Gerard corrects.

I look down my length.

No, not *that* length. Thoughts of my cheating ex-wife took care of that problem. If it should *arise* again, my shirt is untucked.

I look down at my appearance. For the first time since we hired Kendall, I see myself the way others must see me. My clothes are rumpled and crumpled, as though I just got out of bed. Besides washing my hair, the most I've done to groom it the past few weeks is run frustrated fingers through the waves that have grown too long and hang over the collar at the back of my neck.

I head for my seat. "I've been working long hours. I haven't slept much lately." I can't help but sound defensive and grumpy as hell. "Nice to see you, too, by the way."

Gerard flashes a toothy grin at Dex. "I see our Oscar still possesses the same flowery disposition." He sighs like a drama queen. "It's quite comforting to come home to things that never change, even as our company is evolving and is all about transition and transformation."

Leo and Dex roar with laughter.

I could be my usual congenial self and tell them to fuck off. With a smile, of course, since I love them so much. But I don't want to be a dick in front of Kendall.

Maybe I *should* show her that side of myself.

See, that's the problem. I want to be a better person when she's around. And that scares the shit out of me. Maybe showing her more of my dickish side is the key. Since my attraction to her is like a runaway locomotive that just keeps steamrolling down the tracks, maybe it would be best to cause her to lose interest in me.

But *naw.*

Her opinion of me is somehow so important, even if we can't have loud, sweaty, up-against-the-wall sex.

Leticia closes the conference room door, and that's my cue to begin. I take the seat next to Kendall as she taps the keyboard of her laptop. Up pops the first slide. A photo of our new product line showcases the pink highlights that are stark against the black, three-dimensional packaging.

"*Oscar!*" Magnus gasps with excitement. "How very edgy of you, love."

"*Magnifique!*" Gerard agrees. "The pink is very bold."

I eye Dex and Leo. Their expressions say they're surprised, but pleasantly so.

Kendall brings up the next slide, and I give my spiel about what makes this new line different from our others, and also what makes it a cut above everything else currently on the market. As I'm speaking, Kendall quietly gets up and goes to a large box in the corner.

Retrieving several totes from the box, she begins to set them in front of each person at the table. The totes are the same bold pink as the highlights on the packaging. Our company logo is on the front, screen printed in black and shades of silver and gray.

Besides the words Checkmate Inc., which are artfully drawn into the base of the knight chess piece, the slogan for the product line is splayed across the top and bottom of the bag.

More Than a Man...

...a Gentleman.

After she gives a tote to each person, she unpacks one in the center of the table. It's filled with products from the new line. The last thing she withdraws from the bag is a black velvet box with a pink satin ribbon around it that loops multiple times into a gigantic bow. The bow is bigger than the box, but striking, and makes me want to open it.

Slowly, Kendall tugs on one end of the ribbon. Loop by loop, the bow unravels into a long strip of pink satin. The velvet box creaks as she eases it open, and an elegant, gold link bracelet glitters under the overhead light. Dangling from it is a single charm custom made into the shape of our Checkmate logo.

I'm speechless for a number of reasons that are pinging around in my brain. First, I never asked Kendall to put together these promo bags, but it's smart as hell. Something I should've thought of myself. Second, I had no knowledge of the bracelet or what it's for.

Kendall must've read my mind. She lifts her eyebrows and shrugs, as though she knows she's gone rogue. It's so well done, though. There's no way I'm calling her out for it.

I realize my presentation has come to a screeching halt because I'm so blown away by Kendall's initiative. Her insight. Her creativity.

As everyone around the table examines the content of their bags, Kendall catches my eye, notches her chin toward the screen to remind me to keep going, then she sits down next to me to flip to the next slide.

I launch into a discussion about each product in the new line. When I'm done, I turn to her. "I'll let Kendall discuss the promo bags." It was her idea, so she deserves the spotlight. If the idea flops with my partners, I'll take the blame.

She doesn't hesitate. "Women's cosmetic counters in every department store in America offer this type of gift set."

Dex nods. "We offer gift sets, but nothing like this. Pink hasn't been on our radar for our masculine brand." He scratches his temple. "I have to say, though, this is very interesting. I'd love to see how it goes over in our retail stores."

Leo plays the devil's advocate with a shake of his head. "I'm not sure it's worth the risk right before the IPO."

"This promo bag is to win over the board members, not your retail shoppers." Pink taps the velvet box in front of her. "That's why I only had a few of these made." She spins the box around to look at the bracelet. "I called in a favor from a jewelry store owner who used to be a client at my old job. I planned their grand opening event, and I did it at a discounted fee because they were contributing a portion of their opening day sales to a worthy charity. They returned the favor."

Good to know my worthy assistant isn't afraid to use her company credit card. The bracelet doesn't look cheap.

"If you don't like the idea, the jewelry store will take them back at no charge." She closes the box with a snap. "Of course, it's your call, but I thought these gift bags would be a nice touch if we handed them out next week when your board members are here for the real meeting. I know from event planning that people love free stuff. They love to walk away with something tangible." She waves a hand across the items sprawled in front of her. "This is worth pocket change to your investors, but what I've found is that even the wealthiest people don't like to leave empty-handed."

True. I grew up around obscene wealth. Often, the more the rich have, the more they want. My older half-brother is that way. Grant never grew out of the entitled, rich kid persona, and he never lets my father forget that he's a child of divorce. Dad feels guilty for trading in Grant's mom for a younger trophy wife, and constantly makes excuses for my half-brother's douchey ways. My mother plays along since Grant is my father's oldest son, and she doesn't want to rock the yacht that might send my father in search of Mrs. Country Club Number Four.

Yes, rich people are dysfunctional, too. Probably more so. Another reason I keep my distance from the Randolph clan, and I'm so glad I changed my name to Strong. Sometimes you have to love people at a distance, or it's impossible to love them at all.

Leo leans back, his chair creaking. "The problem is the bracelets seem more appropriate for women. Our board members are all men."

Something we should change, in my humble opinion. Women see things that tend to go right over a man's head. Like Kendall putting together these gift totes.

"Exactly." Kendall beams. "Besides impressing your investors, you'll also win points with their wives. A happy wife tends to have influence over her husband. I've seen husbands spend ridiculous amounts of money on an event because it makes their wives happy." She gives me a small smile that says she's not sure if she's overstepping.

Hell yes, she's overstepping the boundaries of a normal assistant. She's anything but a normal assistant, and I welcome her expertise.

I give her an encouraging smile.

She gathers a deep breath and continues. "You could even take it a step further. When the board members are talking dollars and cents and bottom lines with you all," Kendall waves a hand around the table, indicating the key players at Checkmate, "I could entertain the women with a champagne brunch and a fashion show featuring some of the upscale clothing and styles men would buy from your studios. We could give the totes out then."

Magnus and Gerard gasp in unison again, and Gerard reaches over to cover Kendall's hand with his. "Where ever did they find you, love? You're a jewel."

More like a secret weapon. Her idea rocks the fucking house with its brilliance.

"It's summer." She shrugs. "We could make the brunch and fashion show a *Summer in the Hamptons* theme, catering to your board's demographic, and the entire color scheme for both could be pink to match the packaging."

It rubs me the wrong way that our board is going to be stacked with people who will likely have a Hamptons mentality. I've spent my life running from it. Now I've plunged myself, my partners, and my entire company, which is our life's work, right back into the very thing I've been trying to avoid.

Magnus and Gerard are both nodding with more enthusiasm than they had at the Ricky Martin concert where we bought out every VIP seat for our employees last year.

"But the board meeting is next week," Leo says, always the voice of reason.

"It'll be tight, but event planning is what I do," Kendall says.

"Magnus and I can handle the fashion show," Gerard offers.

"It's what *we* do." He pats Kendall's hand again. "Together, we'll make a phenomenal team."

"Out of curiosity," Dex says. "Why pink?"

So far, I've done very little talking once Kendall took over. Mostly because I'm so caught off guard by Kendall's magnificent idea to win the board over by pleasing their wives first.

It's so...Checkmate.

But now I gotta speak up, even as I let my gaze drift over Kendall's pink blazer and up again to snag on her pink lips. A deep pink blush seeps into her cheeks.

Simple perfection.

"Because *Pink* is fucking amazing." My voice is thick and husky, and I emphasize the word pink so that only she will understand I'm referring to her and not just a color.

Kendall's color deepens to scarlet. For a second...or maybe an hour, who the hell knows...our gazes lock. So much is said between us in that moment. Things words can't fully express but are better communicated with a touch, a caress, a moan.

Then she widens her eyes at me for a split second as a warning.

I clear my throat, bringing my attention back to the others around the table. "The fact that pink isn't typically a masculine color is precisely the point." I pick up one of the products. "Only wisps of it run through the packaging. Just enough to tease."

Under the table, Kendall's bare foot massages up my shin.

I nearly choke because I'm beyond shocked at her boldness. Besides her self-confidence, it's one of the things I find most attractive about her. "It's meant to provoke and intrigue."

Her foot slides up and down my leg.

A flash of heat ignites in my chest, spiraling out in every direction. My arms, my legs, my neck. Nothing gets as hot as my cock, though.

The fucker.

"Anything else to add, Kendall?" I ground out while turning to her.

Her smile is confident because she knows I'm as into her as she is me. Together, we've pulled off a professional coup d'état. Her warm hand slides up my thigh to rest against my package, which is straining and aching to be unwrapped.

It's shear agony. It's pure bliss.

"The message behind it is one of bold confidence. Just taboo enough to make a man want it." She recites our discussion when I first brought up the idea of adding pink to the packaging.

My hand closes over Kendall's under the table, but I don't move it. She stills, cupping my swollen length in her palm.

A flurry of excited discussion rounds the table, but Kendall and I sit still, unable to move. Unable to stop.

I'm not listening to my partners or Magnus and Gerard's conversations, until finally our fearless CEO speaks up with a command decision. "Okay, let's do it."

All I can think is that this game I'm playing with Kendall is dangerous. It's unwise. It's forbidden.

So why do I turn to her and say, "Yes. Let's do."

CHAPTER SIX

The official work day is done, and most of our employees—except for the executives—are likely commuting home to their families or gathering at a favorite pub for happy hour. So now that the mock run-through of my board presentation is over, everyone stays casually seated around the conference table. No rush to get back to work. No hurry to accomplish the next objective. Dex discusses wedding plans with Magnus and Gerard. Leo discusses decorating the nursery with Leticia. They're catching up on personal lives like the pseudo-family we are.

Everyone except me and Kendall. We're so quiet we might as well be at a funeral.

Kendall has moved her hand off my boys, but my teeth are still grinding into dust and my skin still burns hot from her touch.

I'm talking surface of the sun hot. Not pansy-ass lukewarm.

Her expression is strained, but shows no emotion at all. When she glances at me, the collar of her pink jacket sags just enough to reveal the rapidly beating pulse at the base of her neck.

I want to kiss that spot.

I want to kiss down her torso all the way to that sweet spot between her thighs.

I want to kiss, lick, and suck until her orgasm floods my mouth.

Then I want to fuck her until she sees stars and begs me for more.

Faster, harder, deeper. More, Oz, more! Just keep fucking me!

I forget my goddamn name as I imagine those words tumbling through her pink, pouty lips as I drill into her over and over.

"Excuse us for a few minutes." I grasp Kendall's...

Fuck it. I'm going back to calling her Pink. We crossed the boundaries of professionalism the second she reached under the table and molded her long, slender fingers around my cock. Referring to her by a nickname is the least of my concerns when it comes to an inappropriate office romance.

I grasp *Pink's* elbow and guide her out of the chair. "We still have to smooth out a few kinks." The very word makes bumps prickle over my skin because the kind of kinks I've got in mind involve a blindfold and handcuffs.

Which gives me the best idea I've had in weeks.

I grab the long pink satin ribbon. "Come with me. I need to handle a few things right away." Like both of her tits, which I've been wanting to see bare and bouncing.

Still deep in discussions over wedding flowers and nursery patterns, no one seems to notice Pink, as she slips into her shoe, and me hurry from the conference room, stuffing the ribbon into my pocket. I have no idea where the hell I'm going. I just need to get her alone and put my hands all over her.

I punch the button for the floor where my lab is housed. When the elevator door shuts, we stand side by side, looking out over the grand rotunda. Neither of us speak. Don't have to because the lust is so thick we both know what the other is thinking. If the outside elevator wall wasn't glass, we'd no doubt already be dry humping.

We shoot out of the elevator the second the doors slide open, and I head straight for the R&D lab, where I usually spend most of my time. Until lately. Lately, I've been spending my time on the executive floor with Pink.

I place my thumb on the secure, state-of-the-art entry pad designed to keep unwanted eyes off of our product formulas. It takes less than a second for the system to recognize my thumbprint, then the lock beeps and we're in.

"You're allowing me into your lair?" Pink teases.

I'm too worked up to answer. I take her hand and lead her inside, weaving through the equipment and machines we use to develop Checkmate products. I look around for a private place, and for the first time since we built our headquarters building, I'm hating the sleek, modern design that's mostly glass walls, which offer zero privacy.

My gaze lands on a secure room at the back of the lab where we store our finalized concoctions before sending them into mass production. It's got solid walls and a lock on the door. I tug Pink in that direction. When we're inside, I flip the deadbolt.

Without a word, I mold my open palm around her throat, her skin as soft as silk against my calloused hand. I walk her back a few steps until we're under a wire shelf that's holding samples of our future products. Another step and she's up against the wall.

"I've spent a lot of nights fantasizing about having you this way." My voice is gravel as my thumb gently caresses her neck.

"You've fantasized about me?" she whispers.

"You have no fucking idea," I say. "And don't pretend you haven't done the same. The way you made yourself at home with my dick in the middle of a business meeting says otherwise."

Lust flares in her eyes, and her hand cups me again, just like it did under the conference table.

In response, I dip my head and pull her plump bottom lip between my teeth. Then I sink my teeth into her tender flesh just enough to make her moan. "We definitely wouldn't be ready to fuck in a laboratory storage closet if we both hadn't had a few dirty fantasies," I whisper against her lips.

Pink's hold on my jewels tightens and she massages with firm, thorough strokes.

"Christ, Pink." My eyes slide shut, and I rest my forehead against hers. "That's so damn good."

Frantically, her hands slip under my untucked shirt, and she fumbles with the opening of my jeans.

"No." My hand closes over hers.

Several creases form between her eyes.

"This isn't about me." I lean back just enough to tug on the belt of her blazer. "It's about you."

One side of her jacket falls open, revealing a light pink, lacy bra. As my fingers work the smaller strings that are tied in a bow to hold the other side of her jacket in place, I let a smile form on my lips. "That color really does look fanfuckingtastic on every part of you." Once more, I let my gaze anchor to her painted lips. The pink lipstick is slightly smudged where I had bit down.

With one hand she grabs a fistful of my shirt and twists. With the other hand, she touches the spot that's holding my gaze. "I bet this color would look even better wrapped around your cock."

I groan and crush my mouth against hers in a punishing kiss.

In this moment, there are no worries about an inappropriate office romance. No concerns over how this could affect me or my partners or our company. No thoughts whatsoever of the consequences. It's just me and Pink and our insane attraction. Our undeniable chemistry. Our uncontrollable lust.

It's been stalking us. Now it's completely unleashed. Circling, colliding. Ready to spontaneously combust.

I yank her hand from my chest and raise both of her arms above her head, holding her slender wrists with one hand. I dig into my pocket and hold up the pink ribbon with two fingers. I've never been into bondage. I mean, some things are better left to the imagination. Or Tumblr. But there's something about this ribbon that's seductive. "Did I mention the reward you're going to get for this idea? The ribbon is so versatile." I brush her lips with mine. "It can be used in so many ways."

Her rapid-fire breaths coat my face and neck with warmth.

"For so many different things." I loop the ribbon around her wrists, then start to tie it to the wire shelf above us. But then I pause. "You made the first move, Pink. Do you want to stop? Or are you ready to play?"

The muscles in her neck bob as she gulps in air. "Play."

Excellent. I finish tying the ribbon to the shelf.

"Then let's play. Hard." I pin her against the wall with my hips. My cock is so hard that she cries out, even though we're both fully clothed from the waist down. That's about to change for her, if not for me. I just need her a little more wound up so I can get her off quicker than I'd normally want.

Let's face it. I'm good in bed because I take my time with a woman and think of her first. That's the reason Pink is the only one of us who's going to have an orgasm in the lab storage closet today. There's a conference room not so far away filled with people who will eventually realize Pink and I have gone off the grid, and they'll come looking for us. Time is not on our side.

I rear back and press into her again, my cock swelling so much that every ounce of blood in my body is flowing to that part of my anatomy.

She grabs the ribbon above her and fists it. "Fuck me." Her words are a breathless whimper.

"Oh, I'm gonna fuck you, sweetheart." I don't unlock my eyes from hers as I unzip her pants, hook both thumbs into the waistband, and slide them down so they pool at her feet. "With my fingers."

Her eyes round in surprise. Then her bottom lip puckers with disappointment, which makes my chest expand because she wants my cock.

"You can have my dick another time, but not in a closet with time working against us. It's not my idea of a satisfying first fuck." The dirtier I talk, the more she shivers, as though she's anticipating. Wondering. Wanting. I slide one hand up her thigh, under the edge of her panties, and find her clit. I circle it with the pad of my thumb.

Her head falls back against the wall. Eyes glazed with desire. Lips plump and parted. Knee turned out to give me better access.

I insert a finger into her pussy. It's slippery with desire.

I smile, my nose brushing hers, and slowly start to fuck her.

"The first time I fill your tight little pussy with my big cock, I want to take my time."

A strangled muddle of sound slips through her lips because she's so excited she can't string two real words together.

I speed my thrusts, circling her clit with my thumb at the same time. I tug down one bra cup, and a beautifully round tit springs free, her nipple already rock-hard. "More pink. I love that color." I cup it and massage, then pinch the hard tip. I swallow her hiss with a smokin' hot kiss, tonguing her in rhythm with the movement of my fingers.

See? I didn't lie about my expertise between the sheets. I really am a good lay, and I've been told my fingers are magical.

"Jesus." She breaks the kiss with a pant. "I thought I was a great multi-tasker."

I chuckle without letting my fingers break their stride.

Her eyes slide shut as her hips start to move. I watch her beautiful face contort with torturous pleasure as she rides my hand. Her tender flesh starts to quiver around my fingers, telling me she's close.

I pick up speed, driving her toward the edge.

She starts to sing, "Oh, my God, oh, my God, oh, my God, oh, my God."

Pride sings through me, too. I love it that she's so into it. So turned on. So unafraid to enjoy the moment.

I bury two fingers as deep inside her as I can, curling them into her flesh.

Jackpot.

"*Oh, my God!*" she screams as she soars above the clouds.

I slow my stride, letting her float on the breeze of orgasm. Letting her slowly descend back to Earth. It's beautiful. It's sweet.

It's so damned erotic.

Not only have I given this girl, who has invaded my mind and my fantasies, enormous pleasure, but I've also christened my lab. Bringing a woman here for personal reasons has never entered my mind.

I don't want it to end.

So, I double down, and speed up my thrusts.

Within a minute she's arching her back and singing again. *"Oh, my God!"* As she quivers and comes over my fingers, she pulls tight on the pink ribbon.

The wire shelf dips and product samples scatter around us. Luckily, I'm tall, so they hit me as I shield her from harm.

We still. Our gazes locked once more. Smiles form on our faces, and we both giggle like naughty teenagers.

When our laughter dies down, I untie the ribbon from the shelf. Gently, she unwinds it from her wrists.

"That was amazing," she says, giving me a shy smile. "At least for me it was, but you didn't get much out of it."

I lift my fingers to my lips, put the tips in my mouth, and suck her liquid sex from them. Her taste floods my mouth, and I wish I had time to taste her fully. Bring her to another mind-altering orgasm with my mouth and tongue.

I don't though, so after-play will have to do for now. Just a tease until we have the time and the place to get 'er done for real.

Her eyes dilate as I suck my fingertips, then put them in her mouth. We obviously have a thing for looking into each other's eyes because our gazes stay trained on each other as she sucks off my fingers.

"I've never wanted to fuck so hard in my life." My tone is guttural like a wild, untamed animal hunting to mate. "But I got plenty out of this," I tease. "This will fuel my fantasies for a very, very long time."

Her Apple watch dings, and she scurries around me, pulling up her pants. She glances at her watch. "Shit. Leticia's looking for us." Pink stuffs the ribbon into her pocket and fastens her jacket into place.

Knowing Leticia's bloodhound instincts, it won't take her long to find us. If she should happen to find us in the laboratory closet, she'll put the pieces together and all hell will break loose. She won't want me fucking up the good thing we've got going with my new rock star assistant by actually fucking my new rock star assistant.

I start picking up the scattered samples.

Pink smooths a hand over her hair. "Do I look like I've just had closet sex?"

I stop and let my gaze coast over her. "You look like someone who rocks at having closet sex."

She swats my shoulder.

I flinch and laugh. "It'll be more discreet if you go back to the executive floor first. I'll be a few minutes behind you."

She fists the opening of my shirt and hauls my mouth to hers. Her kiss is deep, passionate, and lusty as all hell. "Behind me?" Her words are a sultry whisper filled with naughtiness. "I've spent a lot of nights fantasizing about having you that way." She mimics my words from earlier.

My throat goes dry at the prospect. "You've fantasized about me?" I play her game by mimicking her right back.

"You have no fucking idea," she says, still parroting our earlier conversation. "And don't pretend you haven't done the same. The way you made yourself at home with my pussy in the middle of your lab says otherwise."

Before I can offer to spank her for being such a bad girl, she disappears.

I finish picking up the samples and head back to my office. When I step off the elevator, the whole crew is waiting, minus Pink.

"Dude, where have you been?" Leo asks. "We're going to 7th Inning Stretch for a drink. We've already texted our better halves to meet us there. Come on, we're gonna be late."

7th Inning Stretch is on 79th, owned and operated by some of our college buddies from Columbia. They were baseball jocks who didn't mind hanging out with three mathletes. When none of them made it to the Bigs, they didn't sit around whining about the unfairness of life. They got their asses in gear and made something of themselves.

"Sure." I glance around looking for Pink. "Did anyone tell Pi—" I bite down on my tongue. If I give away my private nickname for her, everyone will know. "Did anyone tell Kendall? I haven't seen her."

Liar, liar, dick on fire.

Leticia's eyes narrow. "She said she was helping you with samples in the lab a few minutes ago."

I cough. "Yep. She was." My cough turns to a hack. "But then she left, and I stayed to clean up a mess I made accidentally, and—"

Leticia's eyes turn to mere slits.

Fuck me.

I mean that literally. I need to get laid. My pent-up need and relentless, unquenched lust for Pink is turning me into a babbling idiot. We can put in an hour at 7th Inning Stretch, make our excuses—separately to prevent suspicion—then we can go to my place, where I intend to make every one of her fantasies come true.

"Someone should let her know." I wave a hand in the air as though Pink isn't my concern, when, in fact, I think of little else these days.

"She can't make it," Dex says. "She's already got plans."

Oh. Well, that just ruined my whole goddamn night.

"She'll be here tomorrow with bells on, though," Gerard chimes in. "We'll start working on the fashion show and brunch."

"Leave it to us, Oscar *daaling.*" Magnus loops his arm in mine and walks me to the elevator.

Everyone else follows.

"We'll make you proud," Magnus promises.

I'm quiet all the way to the ground floor. I'm silent all the way through the rotunda. I'm brooding as I step out onto the sidewalk of Manhattan.

The city is already coming to life, anticipation zinging through the air as New Yorkers hustle along, ready to start the weekend and blow off steam.

The same buzz of excitement skates through me when I see Pink standing on the curb. I'm about to go over and ask her to please join us so we can continue her sinful game at my place, where we'll have all night together without interruption.

Pink's back is to me, and she lifts her hand to wave at someone she obviously knows. I stop in my tracks as a built, dark-haired guy, who is about my age and dressed to impress, walks up and kisses her on the cheek. When she turns her head slightly as his kiss lingers against her cheek too long, my breath catches.

Tied around her neck is the pink ribbon.

She loops her arm in his, just like Magnus had just done, and she walks away chatting it up with this asshat. Her head dips intimately against his shoulder as they grow smaller in the distance.

"Oz." Dex snaps his fingers in front of my face. "The car is here."

I look up, and everyone is piling into a limo from our company fleet, the Checkmate logo on the door. When we use a company car, we usually prefer one of the sedans, but with so many of us riding together, a limo is more practical.

Dex climbs in, waving for me to follow.

So much for getting laid tonight. I've just been fucked in a whole different way.

CHAPTER SEVEN

If I said I got hammered at 7th Inning Stretch last night, it would be a gross understatement. Like saying I'm pretty good at chess. Or saying New York City is somewhat crowded.

Or saying I don't give a shit that my assistant left work yesterday with another guy right after I finger fucked two orgasms out of her.

With boxing gloves on, I punish the punching bag at my gym, A Pound of Flesh.

Actually, if I said I don't care that Pink had plans with another guy, it would be a total lie.

I got completely wasted last night. I didn't just see double. I saw triple. Triple images of Pink moaning my name as she came, her hands tied to the shelf above us with a sexy as hell pink ribbon.

I'll be honest. I'd assumed Pink...

Goddammit. I'm going back to professionalism.

I'd assumed *Kendall* would come home with me last night. Finish what we started. Take our time pleasuring each other. All night long.

But *naw*.

Assuming really did make an ass out of me because she left with some jerk-off who let her loop an arm through his like she was his grandma. The streak of naughtiness she has so confidently displayed gave me the distinct impression she liked the bad boy type. Apparently, she prefers the I'll kiss you on the cheek instead of tying you up and fucking you against the wall type.

While I'm sure he was wooing her last night like a Boy Scout, I bet he had no idea what that pink ribbon she'd tied around her neck like a piece of jewelry represented.

I crush the bag with a punishing left hook, sweat sluicing down my neck.

Magnus and Gerard refused to let me go home alone, even with one of Checkmate's chauffeurs driving me. They forced a few aspirins down my throat and made me chase it with at least a few gallons of water. Swear to God, they practically waterboarded me, insisting good old H2O was the best thing to prevent a hangover.

Bullshit.

My head still feels like it's being jackhammered.

An average guy would still be home in bed with an ice pack on his head, begging for a quicker death than the slow agonizing pain that massive amounts of whiskey consumption causes. Not me. I am not a wuss. I am not a pussy. I'm all alpha-testosterone and badass attitude. I typically get up at the ass crack of dawn, but I'm up even earlier today, working it off like a man.

"Getting in touch with your feminine side?" Ethan Wilde—owner of A Pound of Flesh, college buddy, and business associate—walks up and raises a brow.

No idea what he's talking about. "Huh?"

He nods to my hands with a smartass grin.

My gaze follows his, landing on the pink boxing gloves I've chosen from the bin where Ethan keeps a selection of extra equipment in case a member forgets their own.

Shit. I feel my testosterone levels plummeting like a meteor falling from the sky to crash and burn, leaving a scorched trail across the earth.

I shrug, trying to at least maintain the badass attitude. "I tied one on last night." Seemed appropriate after tying Kendall up in the lab. "I guess I'm not paying much attention this morning."

"Right." Ethan nods. "I was at 7th Inning Stretch right before Leo and Dex carried you out with Magnus and Gerard fussing over you."

Ouch. I should've known. Ethan played baseball at Columbia with the owners of the bar, so he frequents the place as much as we do.

"You were mumbling something about pink."

My eyes slide shut. Dammit to hell. I don't remember anything after my millionth shot of Makers on the rocks. No one knew about my nickname for Kendall. I can only hope I didn't give away the truth.

I wave a gloved hand in the air. "It's just a marketing concept we're playing around with."

"Uh huh." Ethan steps up to hold the bag for me. "My money's on female troubles."

I don't respond. I will not give his suspicions any credence. Instead, I unleash the fury of hell on the bag, droplets flying from my sweaty hair.

Truth is, female troubles doesn't begin to describe my situation with Kendall. Apparently I'm not as smart as I've been told because I damn sure didn't learn my lesson when it comes to women who prefer non-monogamous relationships. Jill may have crushed my young heart when she ran off with her Jiu Jitsu instructor, adding insult to injury by paying for their trip to Aruba with my credit card before our divorce was even final, but Kendall and I were just getting started. Watching her walk away with another guy cut deep. This time I won't let it fester for so long. I'm not young and green and naïve anymore.

Another night out at 7th Inning Stretch without my babysitters, awesome friends that they are, and I'll find a gorgeous blonde who'll be wearing anything but pink. She'll want the same thing I do—one incredible night of sex with no strings attached to forget the people who fucked us, and not in the good way.

Then we'll move on.

Except it won't be that easy because Kendall is my assistant. I've given her ammunition to sue me, come after my company, and ruin the IPO.

Christ, I'm an asshole.

I finally stop the onslaught of blows to the bag, wiping the sweat from my face with my forearm where the Checkmate Inc. logo is inked. Leo, Dex, and I all have the same tat but in a different location.

Frankly? The tattoo artist who did the work when we first started the company said three guys getting the same tat in the same spot would make us look like sissies. We were chess team nerds in the process of transforming ourselves to fit our company brand, so *sissy* wasn't the look we wanted.

I pull off the ridiculous pink gloves I unwittingly selected as Ethan gets me a towel.

"Jesus, Oz." Ethan's voice is as concerned as his expression. "That bad?"

I shrug and wipe my face and neck. "Don't know yet." It depends if Kendall plans to use the situation in the lab as leverage.

As I think of the money Kendall needs to help her niece, it's not just my head that's hurting like hell. Pain knifes through my center, gutting me like a fish.

What really sucks balls is that I have no one to blame but myself. I could've resisted. Could've walked away, even after she groped me under the conference table.

But *hell naw*.

I've put myself in this position, and if it comes back to bite me in the ass, I'll be letting down my partners, my investors, and my entire company.

I'm not just an asshole. I'm a stupid asshole.

"I may've screwed up pretty badly." I'm still breathing heavily, and I use the towel to absorb some of the wetness in my hair. "I'm just not sure yet how much damage I've done."

"Anything I can do?" Ethan asks.

He's a great guy with a good head for business, which is why his chain of gyms is expanding and growing. It's also the reason Checkmate decided to partner with him and make personal training at one of his gyms a part of the five-figure package Checkmate offers to transform every aspect of a man's image from the inside out.

Before I can answer, Grace Wilde, Ethan's younger sister, trails through the front door. "Hey, Oz." She waves.

I notch up my chin. "Hey, you."

She greets her brother with, "Hey, lunkhead," as she gives me a knowing wink, and keeps walking.

I give her a knowing smile right back. See, when Grace was still going to school at Georgetown, I happened to be visiting a friend in the area and walked into an Ethiopian restaurant where she was cuddled up with Jacob Rush—one of the owners of 7th Inning Stretch. Jacob and Grace were both shocked to see me, obviously caught in the act. No idea why they kept their whirlwind affair a secret. I never mentioned it again, and neither did either one of them. To my knowledge, no one in our circle of acquaintances is aware of their brief liaison.

None of my business, so I've kept their secret, since it's not my story to tell.

I shake my head at Ethan's offer to help. "Thanks anyway." I got myself into this. I'll man up and take the hit with my partners.

I fist bump Ethan, then go to my locker where I send an SOS text to Leo and Dex, asking them to meet me at the office before anyone else arrives. Even though it's Saturday, I know the executive floor will be buzzing with activity later this morning since we're working on the IPO and the presentation for next week's board meeting.

I shower and head to the office, which is just a few blocks away.

I don't even stop at the corner coffee shop as I normally do. I go straight to the office, and it's still so early that I'm, indeed, the first one there.

I pace the expanse of my office, rehearsing in my head how I'm going to tell Leo and Dex what I've done. How I've left our company exposed.

I'm practically making a rut in the carpet between my desk and the door. I make one last trek to the doorway, then turn around to make myself go sit down behind my desk so I don't look like a lunatic when my partners arrive. I'm running both hands through my hair, which is still damp from the thorough shampooing I gave it at the gym, when I hear a sigh behind me that's as sweet as sin.

"Good morning."

I spin around to find Kendall standing in the doorway holding a drink carrier with two coffees in it. Gone is the baggy look from last weekend. Today, she's dressed in white jeans that are frayed at the knees and mold to her body like Spandex. Her shirt is a fitted, light pink tee that says *Best Auntie Ever*, and her Converse sneakers are, of course, the same color as her shirt.

"You're here," I blurt. I wasn't totally sure she'd show up after yesterday. Actually, I'd already talked myself into believing she'd already retained an attorney and a lawsuit was imminent.

Hell, the way my imagination spun out of control after I saw her leave with a date and the fresh scent of her sex still on my fingers, I had any number of reputable people lining up to vouch for her character just to squeeze a bigger settlement out of me. Other Checkmate employees. Her previous employer. While my imagination is at it, I might as well throw in the National Guard and the Boy Scouts of America because that's how far my thoughts of betrayal had gone.

"Um..." The lines over her forehead tell me she's confused. "Yes." She draws out the word, her eyes darting around like she's missing something. "I'm here. We're still working today, aren't we?"

"Yes." I make sure my voice is cold and neutral. I'm rooted in place, unable to move. Then I remember something Dex said when we were interviewing applicants. I'm more intimidating when I'm quiet and when I'm sitting behind my desk.

Slowly, I turn and go sink into my leather chair, steepling my fingers in front of me.

The silence is deafening.

"Um..." she says again, shifting from one foot to the other. "I brought coffee." She crosses the threshold, obviously to bring one of the cups to me, as she's done every morning since we hired her.

"No, thank you." My voice is steely.

She stops cold. Her eyes round, and her plump lips part.

Those fucking lips. They're painted with a sheer lip gloss that sparkles and has just a hint of pinkish color.

"Have I done something wrong?" she asks, her chin trembling.

And then I see it. The shimmer of wetness in her eyes, and I know I was wrong. I've let worry and anger spin a farfetched tale in my mind.

But she left with a guy. Right after we...

I should ask a few questions. I need to know what she wants from me, especially after yesterday. I mean, I did have my fingers in her pussy, for God's sake. We never discussed any long-term plans. Never promised each other a next time, so I don't have the right to pry into her dating life. Or her sex life. Easing into the subject would be the best strategy.

"Who the fuck was the asshole who picked you up out front yesterday?"

Hell.

She blinks once. Twice. Third time's a charm because the fire is back in her eyes. "Excuse me?"

I tell myself to dial it down, but my mouth has decided not to take orders. "Did you fuck him?"

What can I say? That's how my mouth rolls.

Her empty hand goes to her hip. "What if I did?"

I can't help it. I just fucking can't. I get up, stomp around my desk, and beeline it to her. I leave no more than a hair's width between us as I put my hand at the small of her back and slam her against me.

The coffees topple to the floor.

"Hey—"

I swallow her protest with a punishing kiss. Then I keep my lips a breath from hers. "Because I'm going to have a real problem with you fucking someone else while you're fucking me. It's a deal breaker. And after you let me tie you up in the lab with that pink ribbon and get you off not just once, but twice, I'm assuming we're going to be fucking. A lot."

A throat clears behind us.

Pink freezes, and I look over her head.

"Obviously, we're interrupting," Leo says from the doorway, arms crossed.

"Sorry," Dex chimes in, standing next to Leo. "Actually, I'm not really sorry. This is a real problem."

It sure the hell is because the only woman I've cared about in a very long time has turned scarlet red with humiliation.

Kendall covers her face with both hands. When she looks up at me again, she's clearly pissed. "Real nice." She darts away, pushing past Dex and Leo and runs down the hall to the restroom.

I exhale slowly, pinching the corners of my eyes.

"So, that's what all the blubbering over the color pink was about last night?" Dex smarts off, obviously referring to my comment about tying Kendall up with the ribbon. Even though he's got every reason to be pissed, one side of his mouth is turned up just enough to let me know he understands. It wasn't that long ago that he was in a similar situation.

"Look, I know I've screwed up. I'll figure something out, but first, I need to talk to Pin—"

Leo's scowl deepens.

Dex's grin widens.

"Shut up," I say as I push them out of the way to go find Pink.

"Make it fast, lover boy," Leo calls after me. "Because we need to fix this before it goes sideways."

I flip him the bird because he doesn't have any more room to talk than Dex. He messed up once, too, because he was thinking with the wrong head.

It worked out. They're married now, with a baby on the way. So it's all good.

But Kendall and I aren't getting married. For us, it's only about chemistry. Coitus. Climaxes.

Which is the very problem. And I have no idea how to fix it. I only know that I have to try.

CHAPTER EIGHT

It's still so early on a Saturday morning that most of the lights are off in the HQ building. A beam shines bright from under the ladies' room door, which is at the opposite end of the executive floor from my office.

I knock, then push the door open without waiting for a response, so I can make things right with Pink before more employees show up to work on the IPO. "Coming in."

The marble floors are polished to a shine, and the door closes behind me, creating an echo. The room is empty.

Each stall is closed in from the ceiling to the floor with wooden doors that are stained black. I step to the first stall and *rap tap tap* against it with one knuckle.

No answer.

I move to the next stall and do the same.

Still nothing.

I rinse and repeat to see what's behind door number three. I know I've found her when I hear a gentle sniffle.

"Pink," I whisper, leaning my forehead against the door.

"My name is Kendall." Her shaky voice tells me she's crying.

My heartbeats are dull thuds against my chest. "I'm sorry I embarrassed you. I didn't mean for anyone to overhear."

She opens the door with a jerk. "They did hear, and now we have a problem. *I'm* a problem."

I shift, closing the space between us a little more. Not enough to touch her, though. That's already gotten us into a jam. "You're not the problem." I'm the boss. We've finally hired an assistant I can get along with, and I went and screwed it up in the worst possible way.

"I knew it was stupid, but I couldn't seem to stop myself. I thought we could be discreet." She huffs out a breath. "I really needed this job."

Hold the damn phone. She said *needed,* as in past tense.

"You think we're firing you? That's what you think of me?" My tone isn't as soft and consoling anymore. I'm insulted. I'm incensed. I'm...hurt.

She lifts a silky brow. "I was in the waiting room when you fired an interviewee who hadn't even been hired yet, remember? That's how I got this job."

True. This girl has gotten under my skin, though, and I want her to have a higher opinion of me. Too late, I guess.

I run fingers through my hair. "Look, when I saw you leave yesterday with that..." I so badly want to call her date any one of the disparaging names that have run through my head since yesterday evening. "With that guy..." I give myself a mental fist pump for taming my tongue this once. "I let my imagination run wild." I shrug. "The fifth of whiskey I knocked back at the bar last night didn't help. I talked myself into believing you set me up to be the next #metoo casualty."

Her glossy lips fall open. "You thought I was going to accuse you of doing something wrong?"

I shrug. I'm embarrassed—hell no, I'm ashamed to admit the depths to which I let my thoughts spiral.

I think I mentioned my trust issues. *Thank you, Jill. May you rot in Aruba along with your freeloading Jiu Jitsu instructor, who is probably still living off your divorce settlement. In MY old apartment that happens to be located in one of the most expensive zip codes in America.*

The pig.

The pussy.

The man with half my IQ who has managed to make me lose all faith in long-term relationships.

The same scorn I was just feeling sparks in Pink's eyes. "He's my roommate," she says between gritted teeth.

I'm back to being incensed, and steam whistles from my ears like a boiling tea kettle. "You're living with someone? You didn't think to mention that detail to me before you fondled my balls during a business meeting? If I'd known, I wouldn't have..." I run fingers through my hair again. "I don't take what's not mine." I know how that feels, and I'd never do something so rotten.

That fist that tells me she's just as pissed as I am goes to her hip. "He's gay."

Oh. Hell.

"He's a friend from my previous job, and he knows why I need to keep my expenses to bare bones necessities. He's been kind enough to let me stay with him without charging me rent. He was in the area yesterday and invited me to go to dinner."

Well, don't I feel like an ass. "The pink ribbon around your neck wasn't a cat and mouse game?" I say without thinking. Score another one for my ex. I'm still comparing every eligible woman I meet to her unscrupulous ways.

If I thought Pink's mouth fell open before, this time her jaw virtually hits the marble floor. "Oh. My. God. The asshole stories I've heard about you weren't blown out of proportion. They're really true."

No, they're not. Okay, yes, they are, but I wasn't an asshole to Pink until I got...jealous. Which is something I cannot admit to anyone. Oscar Strong does not get jealous. It's the reason I keep women at arm's length and stay unattached. Uninvested.

Unhurt.

I'm loath to admit that I've become all of those things with this woman.

Pink studies me with fire in her eyes then lifts her chin. "Fine."

Shit. My marriage may have been short-lived, but it taught me that when a woman says *fine,* the situation is anything but.

"If you're not firing me, then it would seem we need each other, right?" She crosses her arms at her chest. It only makes her fitted shirt pull even more taut across her breasts.

My eyes are glued to them.

She clears her throat. "My eyes are up here, *boss."* She points to her eyes, two fingers forming a V.

My gaze snaps to hers. It's so strange to hear her call me that. So impersonal after the intimacy we shared in the lab yesterday.

"I'm sorry. What was the question?" I ask like a doofus.

She rolls her eyes, her frustration palpable. "You need a top-notch assistant. I need a good salary." She waggles a finger between the two of us. "We need each other."

I nod. "We do."

"Will your partners be okay with me continuing as your assistant if we agree to keep our relationship strictly business?"

No idea how they'll feel about it. I only know that I'll hate it like hell. "I can talk to them."

"Good." She steps around me. "You do that." She looks in the mirror, rubbing the wetness under her eyes away and smoothing her smudged makeup. "I'll go get us more coffee." She shoots an irritated look at me, no doubt because I'm the reason the first cups she brought are spilled over my office floor. "When I get back, it'll be like nothing happened between us." She spins around to face me and holds out a hand. "Deal?"

I stare at her hand for a moment, unable to make myself reach for it. No way in hell can I pretend nothing has happened between us.

She taps a foot, still waiting.

Finally, I force my hand to hers. The second we connect, a zing of electricity skates up my arm. She's completely, dead-ass right. So why does it feel like I'm making a deal that I'm sure to break? Or that is sure to break me?

She shakes my hand. I miss the feel of her soft skin against mine the second she releases my hand and backs toward the door.

I reach for my wallet. "You've been buying the coffee. Let me pick up the tab this time."

"No thanks, boss." She puts her hand on the door. "Just handle things with your partners. I'll be back soon." She pulls the door open. "Please don't call me Pink again. It's unprofessional, and we're not crossing that line again in any way, shape, or form."

My chest tightens, and she leaves me in silence.

I skulk...yes, I damn well skulk back to my office.

Dex and Leo have sopped up the spilled coffee with a towel and are making themselves at home on my sofa. They've pulled the coffee table closer and are in the middle of an intense game of chess, using the hand carved chess set my parents had custom-made for me when I graduated from Columbia *magna cum laude*.

I'm ready to take my licks like a man, but I shut the door in case anyone else should arrive. It wouldn't be fair to Pink—I mean, Kendall—for our little laboratory rendezvous to become public company knowledge.

I go and prop my ass against the corner of my desk, crossing my feet at the ankles.

Dex and Leo keep playing, as though I'm not in the room.

My foot begins to bounce.

They each make another move as the silence pounds against my ear drums.

"Jesus, just say something," I finally blurt.

They both focus on me, and the disappointment in their expressions makes me squirm.

"Okay, no bullshit, just the truth." Now my arms are crossed against my chest. "I know it was stupid. I know this makes us vulnerable at a time when we've never had more at stake."

Dex and Leo listen.

"It won't happen again. You have my word that I'll keep it purely professional."

"She could sue us for sexual harassment," Leo says. "We should contact our legal department."

I'm already shaking my head. "It was mutual, and I trust her."

Both of my partners' faces blank.

"Wow," Leo says.

"You care about her," Dex spits out at the same time.

"*What?*" I sputter. "No, I don't." My foot waggles faster. "I mean, yes, I do. She's a good person." I pinch the bridge of my nose. I rarely say that about anyone outside of my close-knit circle. "Fuck."

My partners stare at me, wide-eyed, as though they can't believe I've opened myself up to a woman.

"It hasn't gone very far," I try to explain.

Dex uses one of my old tricks and coughs *bullshit* behind a hand.

At the same time, Leo says, "From what I overheard about the lab and the pink ribbon, I'd say it's gone far enough to get us into a lot of trouble. If it goes public, our investors will abandon ship." Leo blows out a breath.

Dex leans forward, bracing his elbows against his knees. "Leo and I both know what it's like to fall head over heels for the right woman at the wrong time."

Leo nods in agreement.

"I am not head over heels," I say slowly. When Dex lifts his arm as though he's going to cough into it again, I lift a finger. "Do not call bullshit. I swear to you both, it was nothing more than pure animal attraction. I can do this."

Dex rubs his chin. "Misleading visuals nearly sank us twice before." I know he's talking about the PR nightmare Checkmate experienced a while back because of a doctored video that was taken in our 5th Avenue anchor studio...and the unfortunate picture that showed up in the *City Scoop* of Dex getting it on with his future wife on the hood of his Porsche. "Are there any visuals that could leak to the press?"

I rub the back of my neck, which answers the question.

"Shit." Leo slumps back against the sofa.

Dex waggles fingers in a *lay it on us* gesture.

"I took her out for a working lunch. We kissed." I inhale, letting the gravity of my words sink in. I do trust Pink, but my partners don't know her the way I do. "Someone took our picture." This is going to sound bad. Really, really bad. "With Kendall's phone."

Leo shifts into CEO mode. I can't fault him. It's his job and the reason our company is so solid. He grabs a chess piece and starts tossing it in the air, as though it helps him think. "She could ask for an enormous amount of money. We'd have to cut a check in exchange for her silence so our stock value wouldn't suffer at such a critical time. Anyone with half a brain knows that nowadays men in power positions aren't innocent until proven guilty."

"Whoa." I bolt off the desk. "She's not that kind of person. She wouldn't do that." My partners are trying to help with damage control, but it feels like they're attacking a girl who I know in my gut is a stand-up person. So, I'm rushing to her defense. Defending her honor. I might as well be wielding a sword. "Like I said, it was mutual. She's not going to throw me under the bus."

"Wow," Leo says again. "You really are head over heels. I've never seen you go balls out to defend a woman before."

Not after my divorce.

"You shouldn't date her if she's occupying that desk." Dex points through the front glass wall of my office to the assistant's desk. "You obviously care about her, so the chance of another pink ribbon incident between you two is inevitable. What do you want to do, buddy?" he asks sympathetically.

If I had to write up a definition for the phrase *damned if you do and damned if you don't,* this would be it.

"I suppose we could reassign her to a different department, but she's a good assistant, and we need her." I need her. In so many ways. But *naw.* Kendall is off limits. I've gone and let the emotions I thought were gone forever well up inside of me and create a screwed-up situation for everyone involved.

"If it was mutual, then she won't have a problem signing an NDA," Leo says. "She already signed one about the IPO, so I'll contact legal and have them draw up another."

I am not asking Kendall to sign a non-disclosure agreement. Talk about insulting. What bothers me even more is that she might lump me into the *rich asshole* category along with her niece's grandparents. Obviously, I'm wealthy now, but she doesn't know I grew up summering in the Hamptons. I shake my head more adamantly.

"It'll protect both her and us," Leo argues.

He's right, but I still can't bring myself to make her feel as though I don't trust her. My trust issues have already offended her enough, and I couldn't live with myself if I made her feel that way again. She deserves better, especially after the way I spoke to her in the bathroom. I also owe my partners, though. I have to throw them a lifeline because we've always had each other's backs, and I don't want to let them down now. "You both know I've got a trust fund I've never touched."

Dex and Leo go quiet, waiting.

"If this should go sour," which I'm sure it won't because I give Kendall a helluva lot more credit than that, "you have my word I'll take full responsibility and use my own funds to cover the potential liability. Then I'll resign from my position so it won't blow back on the company."

"You'd do that for her?" Leo asks.

Dex lets out a low whistle as they shoot each other a *he's got it bad* look.

"I can't undo what's already done. All I can do is trust her integrity and keep my word that I won't let it get personal again as long as she's working here."

"You sure you can do that?" Leo asks with obvious skepticism. He and Dex both tried the same thing and failed.

But I am not my partners. I'm Oz Strong. Emotionless. Restrained.

"I can, and I will."

"You stuck with us when we fucked up, so if this is the way you want to play it, then we'll roll with it," Dex says.

Kendall walks up to her desk with fresh coffees in hand and tosses her purse onto the chair.

She's beautiful and sexy, and sadness twists and turns in my chest like a tornado picking up speed.

"As long as you're sure," Dex asks, following my gaze.

Hell no, I'm not sure.

But there's no other choice.

Slowly, I nod. "I'm sure."

CHAPTER NINE

Call me sentimental...or call me just plain crazy. For the past week, I've kept in my pocket a pink ribbon from the totes Kendall passed out at our mock board meeting. It's a secret tribute. A secret show of loyalty.

A secret symbol of how much I still want Kendall, even though I can't have her.

I replay the lab scene in my filthy mind at least a thousand times a day, as though a recording has been imprinted on my brain.

Yet I've managed to keep it all business, and we're going to rock the fucking house with the kick-ass board presentation and the fashion show and brunch Kendall, Magnus, and Gerard have managed to pull together like the pros they are.

The executive floor is bustling since the board meeting starts in an hour. Kendall is in the auditorium on the ground floor of the HQ building where she, Magnus, and Gerard are dressing the army of models for the fashion show to entertain the board members' wives.

From the coatrack just inside my office door, I lift the suit bag Magnus had sent over and head to the bathroom, where I exchange my coveted, comfortable—albeit expensive—jeans for a sixty-five hundred dollar Brioni wool-silk blend suit that feels like butter once I slip it on. It has a subtle tonal stripe running through it, and makes me look and feel like a badass.

Thank God for gay men. If we hadn't found Magnus and Gerard, we'd still be wearing ready-to-wear suits from a discount retailer who sells rejects from low-end department stores. Give me a Columbia T-shirt, broken in Levi's, and a pair of old flip-flops any day, but that style wouldn't exactly impress the people we're asking to pour millions into our company.

I pull on the dress socks and shoes Magnus provided. Then I reach for the suit bag, withdrawing a solid pink tie that is the same shade as the ribbons in the totes.

Perfect.

I stare at it a second, then flip up my collar and work the strip of silk into a nice knot. Then I add one last detail to finish off the look by retrieving the pink ribbon from my jeans pocket. Folding it into an accordion pleat, I stuff it into my suit pocket, smoothing down the bulge from the excess ribbon.

When I walk past Dex and Leo's offices to return to mine, Gerard and Magnus have worked their fashion wizardry on my partners, too. Dex's suit is solid black with a pink dress shirt, while Leo is wearing a dark gray suit and no visible sign of pink. When I catch his eye, he lifts one pant leg to reveal solid pink socks. I laugh, but don't stop because my partners are in as much of a frenzy over this presentation as I am.

This moment is big. This moment is important. This moment will define Checkmate's future.

I go back to my office and run through the PowerPoint slides one more time, reciting my presentation by heart. As a backup, Kendall printed my spiel on notecards. She's worried about me since she'll be at the fashion show and not in the board meeting. I don't need notecards, but I'll bring them anyway, just because she went to the trouble. I'm fingering them into a neat stack so they'll fit inside my jacket pocket when Leticia pops in and announces the board members are seated in the conference room.

I'm ready.

"You have a visitor. He came up with a few of the other board members, and he says it's important. He won't leave until you see him." The tension in Leticia's voice tells me I'm not going to like this visitor, whoever he may be.

I don't know who thinks they can elbow their way onto the executive floor, which is only accessible by certain employees and a few non-employees—like Leo and Dex's better halves—but I don't have time to chat, and I'm certainly not going to get distracted right before the most important meeting of my life. "Tell him he'll have to wait," I growl.

Leticia's eyes soften. "It's your father."

What the fuck? "What in the hell is he doing here?" I blurt just as dear old Dad rounds the corner and steps into my office.

"I'm here because I've got something important to tell you, and it has to be *now*," he says, tugging on his tie. It's his tell. Something he does when he's trying to orchestrate or manipulate an outcome.

I drop the notecards onto my desk. I know something's going down that I'm not gonna like. I glance at the clock on my wall. "What's so important that it can't wait a few hours?"

"That's how you greet your father? Your mother and I haven't seen you in months." He pulls at his tie again.

"Give us the room, Leticia," I say without breaking eye contact with my father, Malcolm Wilton Randolph III. If that name doesn't scream obscene wealth, I don't know what would. When we're alone, I ask, "What's this about, Dad?"

He walks over and picks up one of the chess pieces from the board on my coffee table. "I remember giving this to you. We had a Parisian sculptor make it." He examines the piece. "That's how much your mother and I love you."

So nice to have parents who don't hesitate to play the guilt card.

"You're a business man. We're about to have a board meeting that will impact the future of our company," I grind out. "I'm sorry I haven't been in touch, but this isn't the time or the place to play games."

He sets the chess piece down, stuffs both hands into his pants pockets, and rocks back on his heels. "This is no game. I got wind of your IPO."

Shit. We've kept the Initial Public Offering on the down-low to keep vultures from swooping in and leveraging our lineup of investors. Dad's well connected, though, so him finding out about Checkmate going public doesn't surprise me.

It does, however, piss me the hell off.

"With a little digging, I discovered the identities of your investors, who also make up the bulk of your board." He nods approvingly. "Smart, by the way. Your investment bankers who've put this deal together are good. Handpicking the people who will buy up your available stock is exactly how a company should be taken public. Less risk that way. Easier to control your board members so you and your partners don't get pushed out."

Yet Dad is on the board of numerous companies and has pushed out more than a few CEOs and founding partners because they wouldn't do what he wanted.

Something prickles down my spine.

"Which brings me to my point." Dad paces back to the center of the room. "I'm here for the board meeting."

What the...?

"What do you mean you're here for the meeting?" I stand there stunned.

He shrugs. "I called in a few favors from your investors. They're willing to give up enough shares that are earmarked for them so I can buy in and have a seat at the table."

Smoke virtually steams from my ears. To own enough shares to have a seat at Checkmate's table, he had to have strong-armed the other investors into giving up a fuckton of stock. "Don't you think this is a conversation we should've had before today?"

"I can't have a conversation with someone who won't get on the phone." Dad's lips thin.

"I've been busy." I wave a hand in the air. "You obviously know that if you're aware we're going public." Is this some sick game my father is playing just to get my attention? Because it's working like a goddamn charm. "Why are you doing this, Dad? You know I've always wanted to make it or break it on my own. You're a great businessman, so please don't take it personally when I say I don't want you on my board." I leave off the part about how I also don't want him to have leverage over me by owning Checkmate stock.

That kind of leverage is what pushed me into a marriage way too young with a woman who had no concept of what it means to love someone and treat them with common decency. That kind of leverage is also what caused me to walk away from my father's money, my father's name, and my father's cold, stiff embrace, which he considers affectionate.

I've made my own way in the world and forged real relationships with real people like Leo and Dex, who are both easygoing and unpretentious, no matter how big our retirement portfolios get.

Dad's lips purse. "I'll explain later." He starts for the door. "Your investment bankers are explaining my presence here to your partners as we speak. See you in the meeting." He stops and stares at my name that's etched into the glass under our company logo, drawing in a deep breath. He never fails to demonstrate his irritation over the fact that I chose not to ride on the coattails of the Randolph name. He turns and nods at me. "Son."

Speechless, I watch my dad walk past my office toward the conference room.

I've already put my partners and our company at risk by crossing a line with my assistant. Now I've let the circling vultures into our house. Obviously, my father is swooping in to feast on the company we're serving up on a gilded platter.

And I never saw it coming.

CHAPTER TEN

When I get to the conference room filled with corporate suits, I can practically smell the wealth and the zinging anticipation to make more money. Silent expectations thrum through the room.

My stomach churns. It doesn't sit right with me that Checkmate is nothing more to these men than a vehicle to become richer. Yes, Checkmate has made me, Dex, and Leo very wealthy, and we stand to become wealthier still by taking our company public. But Checkmate is so much more than a company to us.

It's our baby.

It's part of our identity that turned three nerdy, chess team kids into men who can hold their own in the real world.

There's little I can do about my second thoughts. The wheels for this IPO are already turning, and we're counting on the money it will generate to fully fund Checkmate's international expansion. All I can do is play the game that I created when I masterminded the public offering of our company stock.

I just never expected the rules of this risky game to be set by my father.

Dex and Leo—who've met Dad a handful of times—give me a weary look.

I give them a look that says I'm as surprised as they are. The fact that my dad is sitting farther down the table next to our investment bankers, who failed to warn us that he was coming today, tells me Dad wanted me to be blindsided.

Leo and Dex greet my father with friendly handshakes and move around the table doing the same to everyone present.

I greet no one. Instead, I stay silent and take my seat at the far end of the table where Leticia is controlling the PowerPoint presentation via a laptop computer.

Truth is, I'm rattled.

I'll sit quietly and process the situation while Leo gives his part of the presentation. He's a fluid public speaker. It made perfect sense for him to open the meeting and soften the crowd before it's my turn to speak.

Me. Grand Master of turning people off because of my abrasiveness. It's my super power. Frankly, I'd just as soon have Leo and Dex deliver the entire presentation because I'm off balance right now. Also, our investment bankers felt all three of the founding partners needed to play a role in this meeting to build confidence in our investors.

I have to stop myself from coughing *bullshit* behind my hand.

There's only one reason my father is here. He wants something from me, and he's going to use my company to get me to bend to his will.

Leticia leans over and whispers in my ear, "Are you okay?"

Hell no.

I nod. "Fine." My voice is a low growl.

She studies me, then picks up her iPad and starts typing.

Leo calls the meeting to order and shifts into speaker mode with the ease of a Maserati. Leticia works the slide show as Leo works the room, but the pounding in my ears drowns out every sound.

I'm numb, as though my spinal cord has been severed and my brain stem is disconnected from my body. I fan out one set of fingers against my lap. It's mine. I know it is because it's attached to my arm, but all sensation has vanished.

"Oscar?" Leo's voice catapults me back to the present, the last place I want to be.

Everyone is looking in my direction, and I realize he must've introduced me.

"Uh..." I stammer.

God Almighty. My mind is blank.

There are only a few moments in every smart person's life when their intelligence does absolutely no good.

This is one of them.

I reach inside my jacket for my notecards so I can give my presentation, but the pocket is empty. When Dad walked into my office, I set them on my desk and must've failed to pick them up again.

Score one for Dad. He used the element of surprise to gain the upper hand. Mission accomplished because I feel completely ambushed.

The silence in the room thickens, and Leo and Dex's eyes grow round.

I know the feeling. I'm a deer caught in the headlights.

Just then, an angel strolls into the room to rescue me. This angel is wearing a stylish black suit with a stark pink ribbon tied around her neck.

Leticia vacates the chair next to me, grabs a coffee pot from the credenza at the back of the room, and starts refreshing coffee cups. The small talk she makes as she pours is obviously a distraction to give me a minute to regroup.

Kendall quietly takes the chair Leticia just left and slides a set of notecards in front of me.

"What are you doing here?" I lean over and whisper. "You're supposed to be handling the brunch and fashion show."

She gives me a confident smile. "Magnus and Gerard have everything under control," she whispers back. "The mimosas are flowing like water, and the wives are happy with their totes and bracelets." She winks. "Leticia texted that you might need me."

My eyes hook onto hers, then glide down to the pink ribbon. "I so fucking do." My voice is husky as a bolt of lust arrows through me. Luckily, Leticia's diversion works because no one seems to notice me white-knuckling the edge of the table.

The pink ribbon vibrates as Kendall swallows. "Then let's do this thing." She squeezes my hand under the table.

For the first time since I walked into the conference room, feeling flows back into my limbs. With this woman at my side, my confidence soars. She flips to the first slide, and that's my cue.

I nail it.

When I'm done, the look on Leo and Dex's faces tell me they're pleased. Dex gets up to start his part of the presentation.

I stand, nodding at Kendall. "Excuse us. There's something in the lab that needs our attention."

Dex starts to talk about the expansion.

I feel my father's eyes following me as I hurry Kendall from the room. I don't even glance in his direction. I need to put distance between me and the man who sired me. I need to be with someone who makes me feel good about myself. About life. About the world we live in.

I need to be with Kendall.

"You were fantastic," she says as we step into the elevator.

It's the middle of a work day, so the grand rotunda below is dotted with people. It's the only thing keeping me from pulling Pink into a smoldering kiss. This is stupid, but I can't control it anymore.

This thing between us controls me. Has since the moment I first saw her. She just saved my ass. Saved the meeting. Saved my company. I'm overwhelmed with the breadth of all she's done for me, and desire crashes through me.

We get off on the R&D floor, I place my thumb on the lab's security pad, then I bolt through the door. I yell, "Everybody out!"

Every employee stops and stares.

"It's just come to my attention that the lab may house combustible chemicals..." I cough. The only thing ready to sponta-neously combust is me if I don't get my hands on Kendall. To hell with the consequences. This woman came to my rescue, and I care too much about her to stop this thing between us that seems to be mushrooming.

That is if she still wants my hands on her. Uncertainty engulfs me until I look at her.

Oh, yeah. Her smoky eyes and sultry expression tells me she wants more than just my hands on her.

"Take the rest of the day off while we investigate," I announce.

The lab is vacated within seconds.

"We're not supposed to be doing this," Pink says. Her skin is flushed, and her voice is raspy with lust and desire.

"I know," I say as I pull her into my arms and slant my mouth over hers.

Her fingers dive through my hair, and she plunges her tongue into my mouth, kissing me as though I'm the only man on Earth who can do this to her.

My body goes up in flames. She's like oxygen feeding the fire that's scorching through my veins. I've been deprived of her for too long. The minutes have dragged by since I first saw her sitting in my waiting room with a large and in charge look in her eyes. The days have crawled by even slower since we promised to keep it professional between us.

But now...now good things are coming to those who have waited. And speaking of coming—I intend to make sure she comes many, many times.

I start backing her to the storage room where we had our first encounter using that sexy as sin pink ribbon. Then I stop. Long lashes shutter her eyes.

"I don't want you to feel like a quickie in the closet is the extent of my interest in you." My body is screaming to strip her and take her against the wall, but she deserves better. She deserves more. "We can wait and do this at my place."

She winds my tie around one hand and tugs me the rest of the way into the storage closet. "Nice color."

In one fluid movement, I turn her so that she's against the

door. "The *best* color." I thread a hand into her hair, letting the silky strands fall through my fingers. Then I cup her cheek and trace her bottom lip with the pad of my thumb.

"Pink," I whisper.

Her lips part to suck the tip of my thumb, and it makes me groan.

My throbbing dick has never hated clothes so much.

She plucks the ribbon from my front pocket. "Do we need this?" Her other hand finds my cock. She cups and massages me into granite.

I groan. "Maybe later." I sink my teeth into her neck, and it sends a chill racing over her. "Right now, I just want you naked." I lay another scorching kiss on her until she moans into my mouth.

She tosses the ribbon to the side. "We don't have much time," she says, worry rising in her voice.

"Dex will drone on for an eternity," I tease. "We can count on Magnus and Gerard to keep an auditorium full of women entertained, so we're good for a while."

Something shifts in my chest. It's betrayal, I'm sure of it. I'm breaking the promise I made to my business partners. My father is up to no good. I just lied to my entire R&D department so they'd leave. It's like a Shakespearean play with danger lurking in every corner.

She cups and squeezes my swollen prick. "Not touching you has been torture." Her voice is ragged with need. "You not touching me has been worse."

Her words and her touch send all thoughts of betrayal, business partners, and my dad fleeing. I swallow her last word with a kiss, searching out her tongue with mine. "That's about to change, sweetheart."

"Thank God," she rasps out, and goes in for another desperate kiss. Her mouth is hot and wet. "Every time I see you..." Another kiss that turns us both white-hot. "Every time you look at me..." Between kisses, her voice is desperate and needy. "Every time I hear your voice, I get turned on. Is that from the Checkmate products you create and wear?"

I laugh, low and guttural, as my hand drops to the Y where her thighs meet. "I'm good at my job, but this—" I do some cupping of my own. "This isn't because of any Checkmate products. It's because you and me together..." I'm not sure how to finish.

I rub the heat between her legs, and she arches into me.

"This is about us, and us alone." A chemistry that defies logic. An attraction that is as inexplicable as it is forbidden.

I cup her face in my hands. This time my kiss is softer. Sweeter.

The passion builds, tossing and roiling like a storm gaining momentum inside of me.

I lean back and take off my glasses and hers. "While I find you sexy as hell in these, they're getting in my way." I lay them on the counter next to me.

She frees my shirt, her hands coasting up my abs. Her touch makes bumps raise over my skin. I shuck my jacket and loosen my tie. She traces my ribs with her agile fingers, then moves on to my six-pack.

She breathes out a lusty sigh. "I want you inside me this time."

"Trust me, there's no place my dick would rather be," I whisper against her throat, then bite and nip up to her ear.

She quakes and quivers.

"Are you sure you don't want to wait? Are you sure you don't want to make me work for it?" I place my mouth next to her ear so my warm breaths wash over her sensitive skin. Her breathing speeds. "Flowers, dating, dinners, gifts. I'll give you whatever you want before you allow me the privilege of fucking you."

"Oh, God, I want you now." She fists my hair in one hand and goes for my belt. "*Please.*"

I chuckle against her lips. "Begging me to fuck you is so goddamn hot." I work the top button of her shirt as she opens my fly.

Then she sinks to her knees.

I hiss out a breath as she tugs down my boxer briefs and her beautiful lips close around my cock. "Jesus, Pink."

She slides one splayed hand up my abs and the other around to dig her nails into my ass. The sting is intoxicating, but it's got nothing on her mouth.

"That mouth was made for this." I brace a hand against the door. My other hand cups the back of her head as it bobs, taking me into the depths of her warm throat. Her tongue licking, her lips sucking. I watch my own private, erotic fantasy come to life as my dick slides in and out between her magical lips.

I thrust my hips in rhythm with her bobbing head as the seed of orgasm springs to life deep in my groin. I don't want her to stop. Her mouth is the best thing I've ever experienced, but the lady asked me to do her, and do her I will.

I pull her to her feet, stripping her down until she's got nothing on but the pink ribbon and a matching pink thong. I expected nothing less. I nod to her spiked black heels. "Put them back on."

She slides one foot, then the other into the shoes.

Not only is she sinfully sexy this way, but the extra height from the shoes will make what I have in mind work better.

I close both hands over her perky breasts and knead them until she's trembling. When I bend to take a pebbled nipple between my teeth, she screams, her head banging against the door.

I trace the line of her panties until my fingers swipe across her wet center. "Jesus, you're so wet and ready."

She nods, her lips grazing mine. "I get wet every time I see you. Every time I think of you. I've worn out two vibrators since I started working here."

I nearly come.

I spin her around so she's facing the door and bend her over. "Hold on, sweetheart. This is gonna be a wild ride." She braces a hand against the door and grabs the door knob with the other.

I flatten my palm against the creamy cheek of her ass and give it a hard squeeze.

She whimpers. "Oh, yes."

I rub the rosy spot on her ass, then squeeze it again.

"Yes! Fuck me. Now."

Gentleman that I am, I give her what she wants.

Grasping both of her hips, I slide into her with one long thrust until my dick is buried to the root in her slippery pussy.

I close my eyes against the white-hot orgasm burgeoning at my core.

If we were at my place, I'd have come in her mouth, then gone down on her until she fell apart. I'd be hard for her all over again and would slow-fuck her for as long as she could handle it before letting myself orgasm the second time. But we're in my lab, and eventually we'll have to return to our work responsibilities.

So, with her hips firmly in my grasp, I dip my knees, withdrawing to my tip, then rock my hips into her again. And again, and again, building speed with each thrust.

Our breaths are wild and unreserved as I pound into her. The door bangs each time my hips slam into the cheeks of her ass, and she cries out the filthiest words, which are music to my ears.

"Don't stop fucking me. Faster, Oz. Yes, fuck me harder!"

This girl is better than a fantasy.

I keep pumping into her, her moans and cries building. I know she's close, so I lean over and whisper in her ear, "Is this what you imagine when you're pleasuring yourself with a vibrator?"

She nods frantically.

"Do you touch your clit, too, and pretend it's my mouth?"

Another frenzied nod.

"What else do you do while you're thinking about me?" I ask, taking her closer to the edge. I can barely hear the banging door over her moans and panting.

"I get off with the shower massager," she says.

"You are a goddamn dream come true." I rotate my hips to increase the friction, and her pussy tightens around my prick, telling me she's close.

I'm on the brink, too, but I don't even have to ask this time. She offers up another morsel of information that pushes us both over the edge. "I carry a pocket-sized vibrator in my purse." Her knuckles are white around the doorknob. "For work."

"You..." My teeth are dust. "You take vibrator breaks instead of coffee breaks?"

She nods. "Yes."

"Because you get turned on when you're around me?" I look down. Her sweet ass is red from the pounding I'm giving her. Her cheeks are spread from the way I'm grasping her hips, and the possibilities of that view are endless. I watch my dick slide in and out, her liquid sex making it glisten.

I mold my chest against her back, so I can whisper close to her ear. "You won't need to buy double A batteries anymore, Pink. My mouth, my hands, and my cock are yours. I'll pleasure you any way, anytime, anyplace from now on."

Her cry of ecstasy nearly shakes the walls. No joke, I'm glad there are no windows because they'd be shattered into a million pieces. Her flesh trembles and clamps around me as she splinters into a powerful orgasm.

My own orgasm erupts like a seething volcano, my cock pulsing and throbbing as she keeps riding my cock, milking every drop out of me.

Finally, I turn her around and press her against the door, laying a soft, lingering kiss on her lips.

"This changes things," she whispers against my lips. "I knew you'd make my body sing, but nothing prepared me for this." She threads fingers into the back of my hair. "I have to keep having you, even though it's reckless."

I let my lips brush hers. "So reckless."

Something prickles at the back of my neck, and I know I've made a grave mistake. We were too caught up in the moment. Too into each other, and I forgot to use a condom.

"Hey." I cup her face in my hands. "I need to bring something to your attention."

She gives me a look that's both naughty and shy. "You're much bigger than average? Because I figured that out a few minutes ago."

"Thank you," I say with a smartass tone. "But no, that's not it." I sigh out a breath. "We didn't use protection."

Her eyes round, her expression turning from playful to serious. "Oh, my God. You're right. It didn't enter my mind. All I could think about was you." Her voice is shrill with alarm. "I'm not on the pill. I haven't needed to be for a while."

This should concern me. Upset me. Instead, I'm ready to beat my chest like a caveman because it makes me so happy that I'm her first in a long while. Sounds like pure agony to me, but the next time we're together, I'll be sure to help her make up for lost time.

"I'm clean," I say. "But I'll use a condom from now on."

When I say *from now on*, she smiles and lays a white-hot kiss on me with lots and lots of tongue. "I'll get on the pill," she says when we break the kiss.

"There's something I want you to know." I lean my forehead against hers. "If our slipup resulted in…say, a baby…I take care of my responsibilities. I'd never be a chickenshit like your niece's sperm donor. That motherfucker needs a good ass kicking."

Cupping my face between her hands, she dives in for another passionate kiss that's all fiery heat and hungry need. "That's what I find so attractive about you," she breathes against my mouth.

"You find my foul mouth and abrasive personality attractive?" I scrunch my forehead. "'Cause I gotta say, that's a first."

"Yes, I find it extremely attractive." She bites my bottom lip. "It's real and honest." She trails kisses along my jawline. "And sexy as hell. We better get back." She sighs into my mouth, and I'm getting another hard-on.

"Yes, we should, because my dick is already in the mood again." I give her one last smokin' hot kiss, then step away to retrieve our glasses so we can both hurry and get dressed.

When we're presentable, she goes for the doorknob.

I place my hand on hers to stop her. "I said you wouldn't need to buy double A batteries anymore. Let me amend that."

Her brows wrinkle, like maybe she thinks I'm changing my mind about wanting her. Pleasuring her.

I'm so fucking not.

"You'll only need double A batteries if I can watch." My voice is thickening again, just like my cock.

As I open the door, Pink launches herself into my arms, my dirty talk turning her on again. We stumble into the lab, our arms and mouths connecting and rubbing and teasing.

A throat clears, knifing through the cloud of lust that's swirling around us.

I freeze.

Pink gasps as she looks around me and starts to straighten her clothes.

"Oscar," someone says from behind me.

I'd know that condescending voice anywhere.

I don't turn around. Not yet. Kendall is mortified, her face as pink as the ribbon around her neck. My father has that effect on people. I won't let her leave here feeling that way. And I certainly won't introduce her to Malcom Wilton Randolph III under these circumstances.

I grasp her chin between my thumb and forefinger. "Go back to my office. I'll be there in a minute." I lean down to whisper so only she can hear. "You have nothing to be ashamed of, so hold your head high when you walk out of here."

She looks up at me, and my heart melts. She squares her shoulders. Lifts her chin. But her eyes are filled with fear and shame.

She struts to the door like the incredible woman she is.

I turn to face my father.

CHAPTER ELEVEN

"How'd you get into my lab?" I ask my father as his disdainful stare follows Kendall until she's gone.

"The board meeting is over. I excused myself from the social after party to find my son." My father is leaning back against one of the lab tables with his arms and ankles crossed.

No idea how long he's been there or what he overheard. I'm guessing he witnessed enough door banging to know we weren't in the storage room looking for extra paperclips.

"You didn't answer the question." I nod to the lab door, where the security pad is located. "This place is locked down tighter than Fort Knox. Who let you in?"

"Wasn't hard to convince the security officer on duty to let me in once he found out I'm your father." Dad flicks an imaginary piece of lint off his jacket.

I'm sure Dad didn't hesitate to mention that he'll have a say over the guard's employment status as soon as the company goes public.

Over my dead body.

"Just another day at the office?" One side of his mouth turns up in a half-cocked smile that doesn't reflect in his eyes.

I adjust my cuffs. "What do you want, Dad?" I brace myself for the *Ask*. I know there is one, and considering he's going to the trouble of trying to hijack my company, whatever it is he wants won't be small. Might as well get it out in the open so I can say, *not no, but hell no*.

He studies me for a few moments, then pushes off the table. "We're going to be grandparents."

"Ah," I smart off. "You've handpicked a wife for Grant this time, and she's already pregnant? Pass along a little advice to my half-brother and tell him to be sure to revoke her country club membership." I rub my chin thoughtfully. "And martial arts lessons aren't a good idea either."

"Don't be a smart ass," Dad huffs. "Your brother's not getting married."

"Grant forget to wear a condom?" I spout.

A tremor of guilt lances through me because I'm guilty of the same thing.

Jesus. That's a first for me.

Dad walks to another lab table and traces his fingers down the back of a microscope. "You know, your mother and I thought the idea behind this company was absurd. We were certain Checkmate's doors would be shuttered before the end of your first year in business."

"Kind of like my marriage?"

He ignores my smartassery. "One of the few times I've been wrong."

"Kind of like my marriage?" I repeat. He was wrong about both my business and my marriage. One caused enormous pride in my life. The other caused tremendous pain.

"We supported your decision anyway and figured we'd bail you out when the company cratered."

"But it didn't," I say.

He shakes his head. "No, it didn't. We're proud of you and how far you've taken this..." He looks around the lab. "This idea that seemed to have no merit, yet you've turned it into a veritable empire." He pulls at his tie.

"Look, Dad." I pinch the bridge of my nose. "You're here for a reason that I'm sure I'm not going to like. You're sure I won't like it either, which is why you keep pulling at your tie."

His hand drops to his side. "My point is we've tried to support your professional decisions."

All the while thinking I would fail.

"We supported your decision to end your marriage instead of giving it another shot."

I grit my teeth. "Before the ink was dry on our marriage license, Jill earned more notches on her belt than a professional escort."

Dad keeps going as though he hasn't heard a word I've said. "We even stood quietly by when you changed your name."

Not so quietly, but whatever. I roll my index finger in a circle, cueing him to get to the point. "What do you want from me, Dad? And what does this have to do with Grant's inability to buy a box of Trojans?" Hell, I'll buy him a whole case for Christmas, because the last thing the world needs is more Grant Randolphs.

"It's time for the Randolphs to draw together. We need to strengthen our family ties so we have a legacy to pass down to Grant's child, his future kids, and yours, too, when you finally have them."

Chills race over my skin, causing the hair on my arms to stand up. I know where he's going with this. "You want a stake in Checkmate Inc. to hold over my head so I'll spend more time with you."

"I want us to be a real family," Dad says with a firm stare.

"Uh huh," I say sarcastically. "I hate to break it to you, Dad, but Grant and I are never going to be tight."

Dad shrugs. "Maybe. Maybe not. There's no way to know unless you try, and you can only try if you're actually around." He goes for the tie again. "If you're around enough, maybe you'll meet someone and start your own family. Your and Grant's kids should grow up together."

And there it is. My dad wants to start lining up potential

marriage prospects again, no doubt from a list of names he compiled through *Forbes*.

"Thanks, but no thanks." Been there. Done that. "I'm doing just fine meeting women on my own."

Dad's eyes sparkle with amusement. "Toying with an employee at the office isn't how you meet suitable women."

Heat churns in my chest at the innuendo that Pink isn't suitable. "Don't talk about Kendall."

When I jump to her defense, I show my hand.

Dad's chin lifts. "You have feelings for her."

"I do." My tone is a warning. No matter what leverage my father thinks he has, I won't let him or anyone else trash talk my girl.

My girl.

The heat churns in my chest, then it slows and settles to a warm glow.

I doubt my partners will feel the same level of happiness I'm feeling when they find out I've broken my promise at such a critical time, but it's done. And there's no going back because I do care about Pink more than I've ever cared about a woman.

Dad's lips purse as he studies me. Finally, he clasps both hands behind his back. "Okay, then. Bring her to the cottage next weekend. We're having a get-together."

By Mom and Dad's standards, a get-together usually means a few hundred of their closest friends and acquaintances. "I'm not going to put her through that. I don't need your permission or your approval when it comes to who I get involved with. I allowed that once. It didn't end well, remember?"

Dad points an index finger toward the ceiling. "I doubt your board would like it if they knew what you were doing down here. Getting involved with an employee is a no-no, or haven't you watched the news lately?"

Funny how my dad is using his power position over me similarly to how the asshat men, who so deservingly get caught up in the #metoo movement, do after manipulating their female employees.

"Show up." The invitation obviously isn't a request. It's a demand. "We'll talk about the future of our family." He pauses for dramatic effect so I'll catch his drift. "We'll talk about the future of your company, too." He paces to the door and holds it open for me. "For now, we should rejoin the others. Never hurts to present a united front."

Except that we're anything but united when it comes to the future of my company or the woman I want.

And now I've got to figure out how to explain to Dex and Leo —my business partners, my best friends, the guys I trust more than anyone in the world—that I've not only put Checkmate at risk by breaking my promise and shagging my incredible assistant, but that my father isn't likely going to go away until he gets what he wants.

CHAPTER TWELVE

I don't speak to my father on the way up to the executive floor. I don't even try to present a united front once we step off the elevator, as he'd expected. He's not my primary concern. First, I want to find Kendall and make sure she's okay. Then I need face time with Leo and Dex.

The entire floor is teaming with board members and their wives, who've joined their husbands and are all holding pink totes. Leticia has brought in refreshments, and the atmosphere is much more relaxed than it was during the presentation.

I'm assuming the champagne fountain Leticia included in the menu, plus the mimosas Pink had served during the ladies' brunch have something to do with loosening up this Mach-5-with-their-hair-on-fire group of investors.

Leticia hurries over and hands a pink tote to my father. "Please give this to your wife. It's a gift from us."

The diversion allows me to split off from my father and make a quick pass around the room to eavesdrop. Every woman is smiling, gushing about the fashion show, and showing off the shiny, expensive Checkmate bracelets to their husbands.

Pink's idea to schmooze the board's wives has knocked a home run for us.

I find Leticia talking to the caterer, and I pull her to the side. "Where's Kendall?"

"She had a personal emergency," Leticia says.

An alarm goes off in my head. "Is she okay? What kind of emergency?" My stomach does a flip because I'm sure it has something to do with the humiliation she's suffered yet again because of me.

"I don't know because it was personal." Leticia lifts a brow. "I told her to go take care of it since the meeting is over and the brunch and fashion show were a hit. She's earned a little time off, don't you think?"

My gait is wide and fast as I go to my office, get out my phone, and pull up the number to the company cell we gave her when she was hired. Everyone on the executive floor has one.

I realize I've never texted Pink. We've spent so much time together these past few weeks that I haven't needed to text or call her. We've been able to talk in person at least twelve hours a day, seven days a week while we prepared for today.

"Hey." Leo sticks his head in the door. "I'm guessing we need to talk about your father?"

"We do. I assure you, I'm just as blindsided as you and Dex," I say. "Poker night at my place?" That's code for *let's play chess*. We came up with the term years ago. Not all chess geeks want to broadcast their geekiness. Our best meetings usually happen over a game of chess, so that's what we do instead of making deals or solving problems on a golf course.

Leo nods. "I'll tell Dex, but let's meet at my place. Chloe's getting so far along that I'm sticking close to home when I'm not at the office."

I nod, tap Kendall's number, and motion for Leo to close the door as he leaves.

She answers on the second ring.

"Hey." My voice is soft and sympathetic. As far as I can remember, Pink has been the only person I've used that tone with in a long time.

"Hey," she says back.

Silence stretches between us, our labored breaths the only sound.

Finally, I say, "I'm so sorry."

"Who was that man eavesdropping on our...our..." Her voice wobbles and trails off.

I put a thumb and forefinger under my glasses and rub the corners of my eyes. "He's..." Now my voice is wobbling because I do not want to tell Kendall that it was my father who was listening to our crazy, passionate sexcapade. But I've got no choice. "He's my father."

Pink's gasp is audible.

"I didn't know he was coming," I try to explain. "It's a long story, and I'll tell you everything, but I'm more concerned about you right now. Are you okay?"

"Besides losing every shred of my dignity, I'm peachy." Her voice drips with sarcasm.

"Where are you? I'll come get you so we can talk."

"I had a voicemail when I..." Her voice drops. "When I got back to my desk. My family came into town unexpectedly. I'm on my way to meet them at an attorney's office." The confidence I love so much is gone from her voice. Instead, it's filled with not only embarrassment, but also sadness.

Obviously, her personal emergency isn't just about my father catching us in the middle of door-banging sex. "Why do they need an attorney?"

A car horn honks, drowning out Pink's voice, and I know she must be on foot.

"I'm sorry, say that again," I ask.

"Apparently, my niece's grandparents have decided they still want custody, even though my sister refuses to take their money. My parents brought her to the city to meet with an attorney."

"I'm coming to get you." I'm already walking through the door, my strides eating up the space between my office and the elevator, so I can get to Pink. "Where are you?"

"Where am I right this minute?" she asks, like she thinks I'm crazy.

"Yep." My father calls out my name, but I pretend I haven't heard and keep on walking. As I reach Leticia, I cover the mouthpiece of my phone and say, "I need a car waiting at the back entrance." Instead of taking the elevator, I detour and take the stairs so my father can't find me.

"You've got an office full of important people, Oz. You don't need to worry about me," Pink insists.

My hand slides along the cold metal banister, and I skip down another flight of stairs. "You're more important to me than all of them combined." Not sure my partners would like it if they heard me say that, but it's true. This girl has gotten under my skin. Wiggled her way into my heart, which I thought long since dead. "Where are you?" I ask again, the dank stairwell making my voice echo.

Her deep sigh feathers through the phone. "I was going to catch the train at Lexington and 53rd."

"Wait there. I'm on my way." I stuff the phone into my pocket and run down the rest of the stairs. I'm in good shape, but our HQ building is several floors high, so I'm winded by the time I slam through the door into the parking garage. A Checkmate limo is waiting, and I jump in.

The driver typically assigned to me is Max, and he's behind the wheel. He knows better than to open and close my door. Just because Checkmate contracts with private drivers doesn't mean I'm a damn pussy who can't manage a car door on my own. I give him the address.

"You got it, boss." Max leaves through the back entrance.

"What's with the limo?" I ask. Max knows I prefer one of the sedans.

"Your company car is getting serviced. The others are in use, shuttling some of your board members who had to leave for the airport right away."

Max and his buddies were entrepreneurs, trying to start their own limousine service. With the rise of Uber and Lyft, they couldn't make the payments on their new fleet of cars. We folded their business into our company, and now they're on twenty-four hour call for Checkmate.

Has to be the easiest gig ever for a car service because we only use them in a pinch, but we pay them for full-time service. Leo, Dex, and I all prefer to either drive our own personal vehicles, walk, or cab it around town. It's part of the Big Apple experience and keeps us humble.

My phone rings, and Dad's number flashes on the screen. I send the call straight to voicemail.

As we approach the intersection of Lexington and 53rd, I spot Pink leaning against the railing that leads down into the subway, wearing her mirrored sunglasses. Her jacket is off, and she's hooked it over a shoulder, no doubt to catch the summer breeze during this midday heat.

"Pull over here, Max." I've got the door open before the wheels even stop turning.

I get out and hold the door open for her.

When she steps off the curb, I snake an arm around her waist. Pulling her to me, I brush a kiss across her lips.

She melts against me. "Thanks."

"My pleasure." I graze her lips with mine once more and let go so she can get into the car. She slides to the middle instead of all the way to the other door. "Where to?" I ask, getting in next to her.

She gives Max an address on 123rd.

What the hell? That's in East Harlem. "That's a rough neighborhood."

Pink shrugs. "This sick grab for custody is a new development, so I don't know all the details. What I do know is that my parents had to pick an attorney they can afford. No matter how much or how little a lawyer charges, it's going to be tight. It'll likely chew up most of what we've saved for the down payment on my niece's procedure."

Anger blisters through me, settling in my stomach like angry hornets.

I'm guessing Baby Daddy and his rich parents are counting on a custody battle to bankrupt Pink's working class family, who are already struggling to make ends meet. Then they'll use the fact that the little girl's mother doesn't have the means to save her daughter from going deaf. I've seen the same unscrupulous tactics in my parents' circle of friends a thousand and one times. It's how the ultra-rich stay in power.

Pink swipes under her mirrored glasses, so I don't voice my suspicions. Instead, I gently remove her glasses.

Just as I suspected, her eyes are red and puffy. I don't know if she's been crying from the humiliation of knowing my father over-heard us in the lab, or if her tears are from the dire situation she and her family are in. Maybe it's both, but I want to fix this. I want to protect her and protect her family. People I've never even met, but they're important to her, so they're at the top of my list of priorities, too.

I place my lips softly on each of her eyes, kissing her tears away. She breaks then, letting her anguish pour out onto my shoulder.

I wrap my arms around her and stroke the back of her hair. "You're breaking my heart, Pink." I feel her pain all the way to my bones. It's soul deep and tears my heart into tiny pieces.

"My niece is going to go deaf because of these bastards," she says vehemently on a sniff.

I want to smile at the fierceness in her voice. It's the Pink I know and love.

My hand stills against the back of her head, and I stop breathing. I can't force myself to pull in air.

I am not in love. Yes, I care about her, but love? *Naw.* We haven't known each other long enough. Haven't taken our relationship beyond work and laboratory closet sex. No way can I be in love. That would complicate an already complicated situation.

"Let's go see what the attorney has to say. Then we'll figure out your sister's next steps." I place a kiss on Pink's hair, and she smells like a field of fresh flowers that grow in the countryside. I lift her chin and give her a kiss that's soft, sweet, and lingering. Her taste is like a warm summer night. "I know you won't take my money, but maybe you'll accept my advice. I've got a pretty good head on my shoulders. I might be able to help."

When we arrive and get out of the car, I take one look at the building and cringe. Any attorney who can't afford better office space than this likely represents petty criminals and corner drug dealers.

"Max." I lean into the car again. "Circle the block until I call for you." In this neighborhood, if the car idles in the same spot long enough, it'll be stripped down to nothing before Max—bruiser that he is—can even get out from behind the wheel.

He nods. "You got it."

The inside of the building is crumbling with watermarks on the ceiling and old, dirty paint peeling from the walls. The floor is tiled with tiny black and white squares that are likely from the 1950s or earlier. Worst of all, the stench of mold and mildew is sickening.

Hell no, I'm not going to let this happen.

I don't say that, though. I'm about to meet Kendall's parents and I'll have to use a little finesse to convince them to use a lawyer closer to my neighborhood.

Finesse isn't exactly my forte, but since I met Pink, I at least want to try to be congenial. With her. For her.

Fuck.

I scrub a hand over my jaw and follow her up the rickety stairs. My phone dings with a text. It's from my father.

You can't run from this, Oscar. I'm not going away.

I silence my phone and shove it into my pocket.

When we get to the third floor, she turns right. "Mom said it's suite 3E." We walk past the doors marked A, B, C, and D, then

Pink stops in front of a solid door that looks as though it's got at least forty layers of paint on it.

E marks the spot, and I step around her. "Allow me." I crack the door and peek inside just to make sure it's safe. A middle-aged man with graying temples is sitting in the small, windowless waiting room. Next to him is a woman about the same age, flipping through a magazine.

Mr. and Mrs. Tate, I presume.

A young lady bearing a striking resemblance to Pink is reading a tattered Dr. Seuss book to a little toe-headed girl who is sitting on her lap and can't be more than two.

I open the door wide and angle my body so Pink can enter first.

The little girl hops off her mommy's lap and throws herself into Pink's arms. She scoops up her niece and hugs her tight. The young woman who resembles Pink gets up and laces her arms around both of them. Kendall's parents join the group family hug.

Pink told me they aren't a family of means. From where I'm standing, they've got something much more valuable than money. They're a family who obviously adores one another. A family who is there for each other, no matter what.

I long for that. My parents have never understood this kind of love and acceptance.

I do not cry. My emotions are pure steel. But this...

This...

I step into the hall and pull the door closed so there's barely a crack. I take deep breaths to steady my emotions.

The door swings wide again. "Is everything okay?" Kendall is still holding her niece, who is sucking her thumb.

I nod, swallowing back the sorrow and sadness that's welling up in my chest. "Yeah. Just wanted to give you some privacy."

She takes my arm and pulls me inside. "Mom, Dad," she says. "This is my boss, Oscar Strong."

"Mr. and Mrs. Tate." I nod and hold out my hand.

Mr. Tate shakes it reluctantly.

They eye me skeptically. Can't say I blame them. Daughter

number two obviously trusted the wrong rich guy who left her with a kid to take care of on her own and no support, financial or otherwise. Now the asshat's entitled parents are trying to take the kid from the only family she's ever known.

A nurturing family who obviously loves her.

"This is my sister, Avery." Pink extends a hand toward her younger sister. "And my niece, Hannah." Pink strokes the little girl's blonde ringlets.

Avery nods with no trust whatsoever in her eyes.

Can't blame her either.

Kendall introduced me as her boss. I'm not exactly a celebrity, but Dex, Leo, and I have been on our share of magazine covers and our names have been in the news enough for Pink's family to know I've not only got money, but also the reputation and power that comes with it.

"I thought Oz might be able to lend some expertise to our difficult situation," Pink explains.

The second she calls me Oz, her dad's brows furrow and his eyes darken.

He *knows*.

He knows I've seen his daughter naked, and he hates it.

Hates me.

For obvious reasons.

"This is family business," he says bluntly. The implication that I'm butting in where I'm not welcome is clear.

"Dad," Pink scolds him.

"It's okay." I shake my head. "I understand." I take a step backwards toward the door. "I'll just wait out—"

Hannah pulls her thumb from her mouth and holds out her arms...to *me*.

CHAPTER THIRTEEN

No one in the room is more stunned than me that her little niece is stretching out her arms for me to hold her.

I've never been around kids, other than attending a few soccer games for Leticia's children. I give Pink a look that I'm sure is wide-eyed and bewildered.

Hannah opens and closes her fingers and leans toward me. It's obviously her way of insisting that I hold her.

Pink gives me a warm smile. "Go ahead." She moves closer.

When I reach for Hannah, she wraps her arms around my neck and rests her head against my shoulder.

Mr. and Mrs. Tate and Kendall's sister, Avery, are slack jawed.

"She doesn't usually like strangers," Avery says. "Especially strange men."

"Smart girl," I say, and mold an open palm to Hannah's back. I don't ever recall holding a child, so I'm not sure what to do or how to keep her from tumbling out of my arms. "If she were my daughter, I'd definitely tell her to beware of strangers. Especially strange men." I repeat what Avery said.

She smiles, making her look even more like a younger version of Kendall. Avery must've had Hannah when she was very young.

With no help from Baby Daddy, she obviously had a lot of responsibility on her shoulders.

Mr. Tate's stone cold look softens.

Mrs. Tate finally says, "It's nice to meet you, Mr. Strong."

"Call me Oz," I say.

Kendall's face brightens.

Mr. Tate's does the opposite, as though he's uncomfortable with such familiarity.

"Or Oscar." I hurry to offer a less intimate alternative. "Either works."

A door behind the Tates swings open and a tweaker pushes through our little circle to get to the door, without so much as an "excuse me."

We go silent, tension rising like the tide. This attorney, whoever he is, won't stand a chance against the kind of representation Baby Daddy's money can buy. I know it. The fearful looks worn by Kendall's entire family tell me they know it, too.

"Please, let me help," I say, letting my gaze shift to each family member. "Kendall won't take my money, but I know people. I might be able to find someone who will take your case pro bono."

Kendall's expression says *thank you* without her having to speak a word.

Mr. Tate crosses his arms over his chest, telling me he's more than skeptical. He's obviously a proud man who wants to take care of his own family.

I admire that, but pride comes before a fall.

I look around the dank waiting room, which doesn't even house a receptionist. If the Tates won't accept my help, they might end up losing custody of this beautiful girl in my arms, who deserves to stay with the people who obviously love her more than anything else in the world.

A wiry fellow with slicked back hair and a suit that might as well have come from the *Brady Bunch* era steps into the doorway behind the Tates. He glances at the file in his hand and reads the name on it, as though he's looking at the case for the first time.

"Aaaaveeeery Tate." He sounds out her first name as though it's eight syllables long.

Oh, no way in hell do the Tates need to rely on this guy. Sweet little Hannah deserves better.

"Please," I say again.

The muscles in Mr. Tate's jaw bunch.

"Tick tock," the attorney says. "Are any of you..." He takes another quick look at the file, obviously unable to remember the name. Or maybe he just doesn't care enough to remember it. "Avery Tate?"

Good God.

"Dad," Pink interjects. "We can trust Oz."

My chest expands as my heart thumps against my ribcage. Her opinion of me means more than I ever thought possible.

"Dad," Avery speaks up. "Let's at least hear what Oz has to say."

Finally, Mr. Tate nods.

I'm tall so I look over Mr. Tate's head and say to the lawyer, "I'm sorry we wasted your time."

When we're downstairs, I hand Hannah to Pink and call for Max. He picks us up within minutes. I open the door and let Kendall and her family get in. Then I lean through the open door. "I'll ride up front."

After I close the door, I jog around to the other side of the limo, the heat from the pavement drifting up from beneath my feet. I slide into the front passenger seat and make the rolling gesture with a finger so Max will lift the glass partition. I've rarely needed privacy when riding with Max, but today is an exception. "Head uptown and drive around until I figure out where we're going." I need to keep the Tates occupied while I make a few calls. Taking them to my office is out of the question because I don't know if my dad is still there. I can't handle my father's petty grasp for control while dealing with something as important as an innocent little girl's future.

Scrolling through my contacts, I pull up an old friend I knew at

Columbia. He's a high dollar divorce attorney who handled my split from Jill. The settlement he worked out was generous for my ex without letting her strip me of everything. In return, he's gotten a lifetime of free Checkmate products and services, and we send a lot of corporate business to his growing firm.

Ten minutes later he's got me hooked up with the best attorney in his family law department. In return for the pro bono work, he'll be a lifelong Checkmate client at no charge.

I also may have to buy him a Porsche after all is said and done.

A sports car seems like a small price to pay for a little girl's happiness, and Kendall doesn't have to know the terms of the deal I just struck with the attorney should his billable hours on the case exceed fifty grand. It will depend on how hard and how long Baby Daddy's parents want to take this fight.

There are few times in life I've been able to do something really special for deserving people. Few times I've been able to play the good Samaritan. I want this for Pink and her family, and I can give her the details if I actually have to go car shopping for the attorney in the future.

I give Max the midtown address, tell him to roll down the divider, and turn around. "How's it going back there? Everybody good?"

"This is so dope," Avery says, showing her youthfulness. "I've never ridden in a car like this."

I laugh. "I rarely do either, but today is one of those days." I wink at Pink.

She beams back, and it makes a spark of delight go off in my chest like a sparkler on the Fourth of July.

Three hours later, Pink and I put her family on a train that will take them back upstate where they live. After speaking with an attorney who has the caliber and clout to handle Baby Daddy and his parents' ridiculous and cruel attempt to tear Hannah away from her family, the Tates' mood is much lighter. They're happy. They're hopeful. Even Mr. Tate's demeanor toward me has thawed. At least a little.

We stand on the platform, waving to her family as they disappear inside their train. A few minutes later, the doors sigh as they close, and the train pulls away.

Pink turns into me, and we stare at each other. The air around us vibrates with energy. The swoosh of a train rumbling in causes Pink's hair to flutter, then settle against her creamy cheek. I finger the soft strands, then tuck them behind her ear.

People pile off the train, flowing around us. Impatient to get to their next destination, as most New Yorkers usually are, they mumble because we're in their way.

Yet it's as though we're completely alone in a city of eight million people. Just me and Pink in a bubble that's meant only for us and separates us from the rest of the world.

I want her. And I know she wants me. The hungry look in her eyes tells me so. Yet I want more with her than just sex.

I mean, don't get me wrong, closet sex was incredible. But I want something she has that I don't. Something I didn't fully understand was missing in my life until today. Something money and privilege can't buy.

I want a family. A *real* family. One that isn't concerned with our image or our economic status. I've got those things already, and now I realize even more than I did before how meaningless they are without someone to love.

Without someone who loves me in return.

"Thank you," Pink whispers. Her warm, minty breath washes over my chin.

"My pleasure," I whisper back, then slant my mouth over hers.

Her arms thread around my neck, and her lips part for me as she sighs into my mouth. Settles into my kiss. Molds into my arms.

Our kiss isn't frenzied or rushed this time, as our kisses have been in the past. It isn't desperate or wild. It's slow. Deep. Thorough. And incredibly loving.

I have no idea how long we've been standing here, enjoying the sweet taste and gentle touch of each other. I can't stop. Can't let go of this moment.

Finally, Pink is the strong one who breaks the kiss. Her nose is still brushing mine, her lips just a breath away. "Speaking of your pleasure..." She lifts a brow and Naughty Pink is back.

God, I love this girl.

I swallow back the words before they slip out. But they're true. I can't deny it any longer.

She smooths a hand down my chest. "How about we go to your place, and we can explore that subject." Her long lashes fall to brush the silky skin under her eyes. "Thoroughly."

CHAPTER FOURTEEN

I take Pink to my brownstone in Gramercy Park so we can spend time alone before I have to meet Leo and Dex. The place cost me a few million, but it's nothing like the swanky apartment over-looking Central Park that Leo owns. Been there done that for most of my life. When I gave Jill our Park Avenue apartment in the divorce settlement, which had been a wedding gift from both of our parents, I never missed it. Not a bit.

This brownstone is more *me*. The *I can live without a trust fund and unfaithful trophy wife* me.

Pink's heels click across the supple wood floor as she sheds her blazer and discards it, along with her purse, onto my leather sofa. Slowly, she walks around the open floor plan, running fingers along the brick wall. "This is gorgeous. Nothing like what I expected."

I toss my keys onto the bar that separates the kitchen from a sunken den. Then I head for Pink and wrap her in my arms. "What did you expect?"

She shakes her head, still looking around. "To tell you the truth, I'm not sure. But younger men who make it 'big' " she does air quotes, "tend to buy flashier places."

Pink still doesn't know I was born into obscene wealth. She

thinks I'm more nouveau riche. It makes me both proud and afraid.

Proud because I know I don't come off as entitled and because I've worked hard to build Checkmate, starting from scratch with Dex and Leo. Afraid because I don't want Pink or her family to ever lump me into the same category as Baby Daddy, who is such a pussy he couldn't take care of his responsibilities and now obviously can't stop his parents from trying to rip a little girl from her mother.

But soon Pink will know everything. The right time will come along, and I'll tell her.

"I bought this place after my divorce. I gladly left the flashier place to her. It was more her style."

Pink's eyes widen. "You were married?"

I nod. "Just out of college." I tap my temple. "I finished multiple degrees in four years, so we were way too young, and it didn't last long." Then I shrug. "I worked a lot because we were in the early stages of getting Checkmate off the ground." I don't trash talk my ex because there's no sense. I went into the marriage willingly, even though alarms were sounding in my young head louder than an ambulance responding to a 911 call. "I think she got lonely, but mainly, I just don't think either one of us knew what love really was at that age." Jill mistook her love of money for her love of me. I was trying to please my parents, and because I did care for her, I thought the marriage license and the fancy lifestyle would guarantee her loyalty. We were both wrong.

I tuck a strand of hair behind Pink's ear. "Now I try to stay a little more under the radar."

She lifts a silky brow. "This neighborhood is what you call under the radar?"

I chuckle. "Wait 'till you see where Leo lives. This place is definitely under the radar compared to Leo's apartment." I guess she's right about the nouveau riche. Neither of my partners came from money. They aren't assholes about their success, but Leo definitely lives flashier than I do. Just like me, Dex traded his swanky apart-

ment for a brownstone when he met Ava, but he dresses like a *GQ*
model, which I so don't.

"Speaking of," I pull Pink close, and she flattens both palms
against my chest, "I've got to meet my partners later, but we have a
few hours." I let my gaze coast over her pretty face, taking in the
long, silky lashes, the defined cheekbones, the plump lips. I can't
look away from those lips. "How would you like to spend them?"

Her eyes turn smoky, mirroring my thoughts.

One of Pink's hands descends down to my belt, but I engulf it
with mine. "Our strategy is going to be a little different this time."
We're not in a laboratory closet, and I intend to take my time.
Make it last.

"You've developed a strategy?" She tilts her head to the side.

"Uh huh." I bring her fingers to my lips and shower them with
kisses.

"That must've taken a lot of thought." Her voice is breathy.

"Hours upon hours of thought." My words are a promise. A
promise that won't go unfulfilled.

Her pupils expand to black marbles, and the tip of her tongue
slips from her mouth to trace her bottom lip, as though she's imag-
ining the possibilities. "In that case, it would be a shame to let the
time and energy you've spent go to waste. Testing this strategy of
yours sounds like an excellent use of the next few hours."

She squeaks as I cup her ass cheeks and lift her off the ground.
Her legs anchor around my hips, and her arms circle my neck.

As I trek down the hall toward my bedroom, she bites and nips
at my neck. My skin prickles, and my dick springs to life. Not that
it isn't always standing at attention when I'm with Pink. She grinds
against me, feathers hot kisses up to my ear, tugging my earlobe
between her teeth. Her warm, moist breath washes across my ear
and over my neck.

"Jesus, woman," I breathe out. "You have no idea what you do
to me."

She grinds her pussy against my cock again. "I've got a pretty
good idea." She laughs against my ear.

When we get to my room, I don't put her down.

We're both breathing hard and grinding harder by the time I finally break the kiss.

I set her down, trailing a finger along her neck, over her collarbone, and down between her breasts. "Want to know the first part of my strategy?"

She tilts her head to the side. "Do tell."

"You stripping for me," I say. I'm desperate to feel her bare skin rub against mine, but we've done the *hurry up and fuck me 'cause we don't have much time* thing twice already in my lab. This time will be different. I want to make love to her. I want it to last.

Something shifts in my chest. I don't just want the sex to last. I want *us* to last. See where it might lead. I know it was stupid to get involved with my assistant, but my partners spoke the truth when they said they'd both fallen for the right girl at the wrong time.

I know Pink won't screw me over. Somehow, I just know, and it's the first time I've been willing to trust a woman since my ex chewed my heart into tiny pieces, one agonizing bite at a time. So this round with Pink will be special. She'll know I care. She'll understand I'm not just using her body. She'll feel worshipped when I'm done.

Her lashes flutter downward. "Okay." She pushes on my shoulders, and I take a step back. "But you first." She sits on the edge of my oversized king bed, crosses her legs, and braces her hands behind her. "We've had sex twice, but I still haven't seen you naked."

True. Both times we were together in my lab, there wasn't time for both of us to bare all.

I give her a cocky smile and take another step back. One hand goes to my tie. Holding her gaze, I start at the bottom of the long piece of pink silk and let my fingers drift up until I reach the knot. Slowly, I loosen it until I can slip it over my head.

I place it around her neck. "This color looks so fantastic on you, I want to see you in nothing but this."

She reaches for my belt, but I step out of reach.

"Tsk, tsk." I release one cuff, then move to the other. "It'll be much more interesting if we don't rush this time. I promise." I go to work on the buttons of my shirt. Starting at the top, I slowly work to free each one, exposing more of my chest and abs as my shirt falls open wider with each flick of my fingers against the mother of pearl circles.

I shed the shirt, tossing it to the side.

Her smoldering gaze licks over my bare torso, making my skin prickle and heat. Then her eyes snag on my forearm where I'm inked with the Checkmate logo. Then her gaze slides up to my biceps.

Like a stupid, high school jock, I flex. I can't help it. I just fucking can't. The way she looks at me says she likes what she sees. I was a prep school kid who leaned toward nerdy. Maybe not as much as my two partners. Hell, my parents were too concerned with image to let me become a total geek, even though I was a science wizard and kept my nose in a book far more than I cared to play sports. But I'm proud of the healthy and muscular physique I've spent years building in the gym.

Right about now, I'm especially proud that Pink obviously appreciates a six-pack.

"I love a tattoo that has special meaning," she says.

"It's the only kind I would ever get." When my hands fall to my belt, she licks her lips.

"Do you have any?" I doubt it because I've seen Pink naked... mostly...and haven't noticed a tat. Then again, I was kinda busy both times she had her clothes off around me.

She shakes her head. "Never found one with enough meaning."

"Virgin skin," I taunt, kicking off my shoes and pants so that I'm down to my boxer briefs. "My favorite kind."

Pink crooks a finger at me to come closer.

God, I love how this woman thinks. I take a step closer, but she keeps crooking that finger. One more step puts me close enough for her to open her legs and circle her arms around to my ass. With a dip of her head, she uses her teeth and tongue to kiss and nip along my length.

Talk about pitching a tent.

I groan, stabbing my fingers into her hair as her hot, moist breaths make the friction of my briefs against my cock almost unbearable. Gently, I massage her hair, enjoying the warmth of her mouth until I can't take it another second.

I step back, hook both thumbs into my waistband and slide my boxers down so I can send them sailing in the direction of my pants.

Her mouth turns up into a sultry smile as she drinks in the sight of my package like a tall, savory cocktail. Pun intended.

I crook a finger at her this time. "Your turn." She stands up and reaches for my tie that's still around her neck.

I circle her wrist. "Leave it."

As she starts to slowly shed her clothes one piece at a time, I lie back on my bed and sink into the plush comforter with my hands laced behind my head.

"I've never actually stripped." Pink is down to her panties and bra. And the tie. The tie is fucking unforgettable.

Good. I don't want another man's eyes on her bare flesh. "You're doing just fine," I encourage her.

She reaches behind her back to fiddle with her bra hook. "I've been tempted to take pole dancing lessons, though." With a few sexy bats of her lashes, she says, "For the exercise."

My gaze drifts over her flat belly, her waist that dips in then flares into nice full hips. She's exquisite. "Seems to me you're doing just fine in the fitness department, too. I'm down for pole dancing, though. As long as I'm the only one watching."

Her bra springs loose and she cups her own tits and massages, the lace moving and shifting over the lovely mounds. One strap slides down her arm, and I let a moan slip through my lips.

"You like to watch, don't you?" She's toying with me, and I flipping love it.

"Sweetheart, I like to watch *you*." My dick throbs. "It's a goddamn turn on."

Her big brown eyes glide down my torso to my pulsing prick. "I can tell." She slides the other strap off and holds her bra to the side, letting it dangle from an index finger. Two beautiful breasts greet me with perfectly pink and pebbled nipples.

Hell yes, I'll watch this woman with her pocket rooster or her private strip tease or her pole dancing number, especially with those beautiful tits bouncing for only me to see.

When she's completely bare-ass naked—with the exception of my tie, which hangs between the valley of her breasts—she starts at my feet and climbs up my body.

As much as I'd love to have her mouth on my cock again, I don't let her linger there. Instead, I roll her onto her back and cover her body with mine in one fluid motion.

The flame of desire flares, heating the air around us. I lower my head and take her mouth in a kiss that's hot and wet, and oh, so sultry. A slow burn starts low in my belly and grows hotter with each swipe of our tongues, each sexy sound that we're both making.

I'm wound tighter than a clock that's ready to go off.

This isn't the first time we've been skin to skin, but somehow this time is different, and we both seem to know it. She circles my waist with her legs, pulling me closer so that my tip is at her wet entrance. Need spirals through me, but I beat back the urge to plunge into her depths.

I kiss down her neck, closing my mouth around a perky tit.

She hisses in a breath and arches into me.

I suckle it until she's moaning and writhing under me, and it feels so amazing that I don't want to stop. But I do and move to the other gorgeous breast to lick and suck until she cries out my name. That's my cue to go lower, grazing kisses along her belly. When I circle her belly button with my tongue, her skin turns hot, yet she's shivering.

I settle between her firm legs, placing a kiss on the inside of one thigh, then the other. Then I breathe in her scent and let out a sigh of pure ecstasy.

She fists my hair in her hands, the anticipation obviously working her up into a ball of needy, hungry lust.

That's my cue to dive in, and I lick straight up her center, tonguing her nub. "So good," I whisper against her wet pussy, then I go in for more.

She shudders and shakes, and sinks a set of nails into one of my shoulders.

I circle my tongue, finding a rhythm that mouth fucks her to the edge.

"*Oz.*" She arches into me. "That's so...so good."

"I know, baby." I lick, suck, and circle, then I insert two fingers into her depths and curl them.

She cries out and explodes into a window-shattering orgasm. It's so sensual and sexy, and so goddamn erotic that I almost come myself. But hell no. A real man can wait until his lady has had two, three, ten climaxes to his one.

I kiss up her body until my pulsing dick is nestled at the entrance of her slick center again. I don't angle for a more creative position. I've already finger fucked her to an orgasm with her hands tied, then taken her from behind until her shouts of pleasure practically rocked Checkmate's HQ building like an earthquake. This time I opt for the traditional missionary style, so I can slow fuck her while she looks into my eyes.

I brace an elbow next to her head and place my other hand at the back of her thigh, just above the knee. Then I lift her leg to spread her wide and circle my hips to tease her even more.

Her eyes flutter shut.

"Look at me." For me, this isn't just another fuck. I want her to know how special she is to me.

She opens her eyes again, anchoring them to mine.

"Good girl," I say, sliding in until I'm fully seated to my hilt.

She moans and arches and closes her eyes again.

"Look at me," I repeat.

She does, and I say, "I want to see you while we're making love."

Her eyes are glazed, but she does what I ask and doesn't shut them as I start to move inside of her.

I lift my hips, withdrawing to my tip, then sink into her again.

Her nails rake across my back, and her breathing grows more and more ragged as I withdraw and thrust, withdraw and thrust.

I keep my rhythm to a slow cadence to draw out the moment, so the pleasure won't end too quickly. Every time I bury myself inside her hot pussy, I grind my teeth, trying to control my own hungry need.

"I want you all the fucking time," I whisper against her mouth.

She bites my bottom lip. "You can have me all the fucking time."

That topples my self-control, and I pick up speed, delving into her sweetness.

"*Oz.*" My name tumbling through her lips on a desperate sigh is the best damn thing I've ever heard. "God, that's so...so good."

The seed of orgasm springs to life as my balls tighten and my dick goes from hard to granite. "So damn good," I ground out.

She fills both palms with my ass cheeks and pulls me deeper every time I rock my hips into hers. Her nails bite into my flesh, and the sting is so sweet and sexy that I'm holding on to my sanity by a thread.

I tug her leg higher, opening her so wide as I ride her fast and hard. It's so damn good that I forget my goddamn name. Our fit is pure perfection, and I wonder how I let my heart go on lockdown for so long because of a woman I married way too young before I really knew what love was. Her betrayal shouldn't have mattered for so long. Shouldn't have kept me from feeling, living, or loving for all those years.

It was so damn wrong.

But this is so fucking right.

I shift and circle my hips in the opposite direction, increasing the friction.

Pink cries out, "Oz!" And then she shatters in my arms, her pussy quivering around my cock so that I'm tumbling over the edge along with her. We're falling, falling, falling, and it's so incredible that we're falling together as my cock pumps my orgasm into her.

I still. Rest my forehead against hers, our breathing still heavy. Her beautiful, full breasts brush against me with each rise and fall of her chest. I swallow, realizing I've made another mistake, and my whole body goes rigid.

"What?" she whispers.

I lift my head to look down at her. A fine sheen of moisture glistens over her face.

I let a long, slow breath release as I stroke a damp strand of hair off her forehead. "I forgot to use a condom again."

Her eyes round, and she sucks in a breath. "Oh, God."

Bare is something I just don't do because it's irresponsible.

Somehow, though, I don't see it that way with Kendall. In fact, the thought of her belly growing round with a little Oz...or a little Ozette...doesn't bother me in the least.

CHAPTER FIFTEEN

Me and Pink have gone several more rounds, and I've lost all track of time. We're sweaty and spent, and we doze while wrapped in each other's arms, snuggled underneath the plush comforter on my bed.

With her head on my chest, she circles a finger through the smattering of hair between my pecs. "That was incredible. You've ruined me for life."

Fine by me. Call me selfish, but if she never wants another man but me after today, I'm good with it. I stroke a hand down her silky hair, letting the long strands fall through my fingers. "Closet sex was incredible, but having a bed and a lot of time was mind-blowing."

She shifts to look up at me. "Don't you have to meet your partners?"

I groan and look over her so I can see the clock on the bedside table. "Damn. I'm late. I really hate my partners right now."

Pink laughs. "Come on," she says, raising to an elbow. "Go get cleaned up."

I shake my head. "No time to clean up. I'll have to go as I am."

Her brow quirks. "Naked?"

I laugh. "Without a shower." I swat her bare rump. "We can shower together when we get back."

"We?" Her expression blanks.

"Yep." I roll out of bed. "Get dressed. You're coming with me." We're a package deal now, and I need to let my partners know. "On the way back, we can swing by your place and pick up an overnight bag. Then we can get something to eat." I pull on the same clothes I wore earlier. Seems only fair since Pink has to put her work clothes back on.

On the ride over I text Leo and Dex to tell them Kendall will be with me. I also request Chloe sit in on the meeting. We're gonna need our PR account rep's input now that we're staring down the barrel of my father's manipulative corporate genius. He's got us zeroed in with his mad skills at strong-arming people.

During the drive to Leo's, I stroke Pink's thigh to keep the mood going and turn on soft music, which filters through the speakers of my Tesla.

When we're standing in front of Leo's door, Pink gives me a wide-eyed look. "You weren't kidding about your partner's apartment. If this isn't flashy, I don't know what would be."

My fingertips massage the small of her back. "My partners are even more down to earth and real than I am, so don't worry." They were born that way. Grew up that way. I had to figure things out on my own once I was old enough to realize my parents' elitist way of doing things was bullshit.

I reach for the bell, but the door swings wide. Leo waves us in. "Doorman called and said you were on your way up."

Pink shoots a look at me that says *Down to earth? Really?* Any apartment building with a doorman, especially in this neighborhood, is going to cost a fortune, so I see her point.

I wink and press my hand into the small of her back so she'll go inside.

Dex is at the dining room table, resetting the chess board. "I just kicked Leo's ass. You're next."

They might both want to kick my ass after I tell them my dad is likely going to use our company as leverage to get me to do what he wants. "Later. Let's talk first."

Dex stills. "I knew the situation was serious when our unexpected guest showed up and was so cozy with our other investors and our bankers, but it must be bad if you don't want to play chess. We always talk *while* we're playing chess. It's our thing."

"Not tonight." I motion for Pink to follow me into Leo's living room, which has one glass wall running the length of the room. It's getting dark, and the lights of Manhattan's skyline twinkle in the distance like diamonds scattered across a swath of dark velvet.

A subtle gasp slips through Pink's lips at the view.

I squeeze her hand when no one is looking and pull her down next to me on Leo's modern leather sofa.

Before anyone else joins us, Leo hurries to take a seat on the edge of a chair to my right and says, "I don't mean to embarrass you, Kendall, but I'm assuming you're both here to tell us you've broken your word? Because we already knew that before we even left HQ earlier today."

"It's that obvious?" I know that it is, but I guess I'm in a little bit of denial about my transgressions.

"Well." Leo rubs his chin. "You two disappeared together while the meeting was still in progress." He looks at me and drops his voice. "When you rejoined us, the pink ribbon in your pocket was gone." He lowers his voice yet another notch. "And you both smell like walking sex. Dude, you own a shower, right?"

Remember when I said smart people can be stupid sometimes? This is one of those times.

When I look at Pink, her face has gone up in flames. I give her a half-smile that says I'm sorry.

Dex joins us, taking a seat across the coffee table from me and Pink.

I drape my arm around the sofa at her back, not trying to hide our intimacy. No sense pretending. That genie is so far out of the damn bottle we might as well pull up an extra chair for it and start making wishes.

I'm relieved my partners don't seem upset about my broken promise to not get involved with my assistant. I guess they've walked a few million miles in my shoes and understand when a guy meets that special woman—the one who sets his broken world right—he's a goner.

That would be me—a total fucking goner.

"Kendall," Leo focuses on her. "You do realize this puts Checkmate in a less than ideal situation, especially right before our company goes public?"

So much for my partners walking a million miles in my shoes.

I all but growl. "Leo—"

"It's okay," Kendall interrupts me. "You know Oz better than I do, and you know he'd never pressure me. This was not only mutual, but I was more the aggressor than him."

"Would you sign a non-disclosure agreement to that effect?" Dex asks.

"That's enough." I jump to Pink's defense.

She holds up a hand. "I'd be happy to." She turns a definitive look on me. "That's final. Now, let's move on. I think you and your partners have bigger problems than me signing a form."

I draw in a deep breath. Finally, I nod. "My dad didn't say anything to you two after I left?" I ask Leo and Dex, flexing my fingers into my thigh.

Leo shakes his head. "Not a word. He wouldn't tell us why he was there, and neither would our investment bankers. All he said was that he was there at the behest of the other investors and the extent of his involvement with Checkmate's IPO would depend on you." Leo hitches his chin at me.

I scrape a hand over my jaw, the stubble pricking my fingers. I shaved this morning for the meeting, but I've got a shadow of whiskers peeking through by this time of the evening.

Chloe waddles in from the kitchen, with Ava trailing behind her.

"Hey." I get up and give her a brotherly peck on the cheek. "You look fantastic."

"I look like an Oompa Loompa." She introduces herself to Pink. "Nice to meet you, Kendall." Then she sits in a way that says it's a long way down into the chair.

Leo runs to help her.

"You realize there's no hope of me getting up again? I'll give birth right here unless you can get a small crane up the elevator."

I give Ava the same brotherly peck, then she sits on the arm of Dex's chair, draping herself around him. The mammoth engagement ring on her finger glitters under the lights.

I don't pause for more pleasantries. Pleasantries aren't in my nature. Instead, I dive right into the sordid details of my father's visit to my lab. Okay, I left out the door-banging sex, but that kind of goes without saying.

"What do you think he wants?" Dex asks.

I blow out a frustrated breath. "I don't think it's only about trying to bring our family closer."

Dex's laugh is laced with sarcasm. "Using your company as leverage doesn't inspire family loyalty. My parents are asshats, too, so I'm not surprised your dad thinks this is the way to build familial bonds."

"My brother is involved somehow," I say, thinking.

Dex and Leo both mumble obscenities under their breaths. Well deserved, as far as I'm concerned. Grant and I might share paternal DNA, but he isn't my family. The few times my partners have had the misfortune of meeting Grant, their takeaway was to ask how it was scientifically possible for the two of us to be even remotely related.

"I don't think my dad is being completely honest about that either. My half-brother is going to be a father." I explain that my dad is using my brother's unborn child as an excuse to bring me back into the fold. "My intellect tells me there's more to the story than my father is letting on."

"I think your instincts probably have something to do with it, too." Kendall's been quiet until now, and all eyes turn to her.

Chloe nods. "I agree." She rubs her tummy.

For a moment, I'm swept away watching Chloe. I picture Kendall pregnant with my child. A newborn nursing at her breast. A baby crying in my arms as I walk the floor in the middle of the night so Kendall can sleep.

My chest squeezes with longing at that perfect picture.

"Oz." Leo waves a hand as close to my face as he can get. It knocks me back into the present.

Pink leans over and whispers in my ear, "Are you okay, babe?"

Babe. The sound of that is even more beautiful than her screaming my name in the middle of a window-shattering orgasm.

"I'm fine." I clear my throat.

Dex lifts his arm, and I know he's going to cough *bullshit* behind it.

"I'm *fine,*" I repeat, glaring at him.

He drops his arm with a smartass grin.

"The question is, what does he want?" Kendall says.

Chloe chimes in. "And how do we get him to tell us?"

Now it's Ava's turn. "Don't forget that whatever it is he wants, it's something you're probably not going to be on board with, Oz."

This is why Checkmate needs women on the board. They're wiser than all of us dudes combined.

"I've got an idea." I hold up a finger. "Dad is expecting me to bring Kendall to their cottage in the Hamptons next weekend for a party."

Her grip on my hand contracts. I know she's reacting to the fact that my parents live in the Hamptons, a fact I've failed to mention until now.

I engulf her hand with both of mine, running soothing fingers along the knuckles.

"Since he's obviously issuing a veiled threat to use Checkmate as leverage, I think we should all go." I'm not being a chickenshit. My partners know I'm not afraid to stand toe to toe with my dad. It's just that there's power in numbers.

"Except you, Chloe," I say. "I understand if you can't make it."

"Are you kidding?" She scoffs. "There are hospitals on Long Island, and I'll bring my packed bag along, just in case. I wouldn't miss this for the world." She gives Leo a deadpan stare. "Can you find a crane by then?"

"We're in," Ava answers for Dex, too.

This is why I love these people. They're my friends. My *family*. The people who really do present a united front with me and actually mean it, instead of it being a phony act for appearance's sake.

"Just to be clear..." Kendall leans forward. "From what you've said, Oz, it sounds like your dad is playing some sort of game with you and your company."

That's my father. He sees business, company takeovers, and leveraged buyouts as a game. He doesn't usually make the first move unless he knows he can win. "Yes. I'd have to agree. The problem is this game he's playing is with our life's work." I glance around the room at my two partners. We've been in this together since day one, and I can't let my dad screw with that.

Kendall smiles. "That's my point." She offers a pointed look at me, then Dex, then Leo. "Don't forget who you are."

"Ahhhh." Ava nods approvingly, like she completely gets where Kendall is going with this.

Chloe follows suit with a dainty opera-ish clap. "Brava."

I so don't get it. I look at Dex and Leo to throw me a lifeline, but their looks tell me they're just as confused as I am.

How many geniuses does it take to understand women? Especially the women who've captured our hearts, because they seem to be outwitting us all? "I don't understand."

Kendall pinches my cheek. "Oh, aren't you three so cute and clueless."

Chloe and Ava belly laugh.

"Glad you three are so entertained," Leo says blandly.

"Care to clue in the clueless?" Dex asks with noticeable irritation. Then he squeezes Ava's thigh.

"You three are master chess players, right? Champions," Pink says. When none of us can figure out the meaning of her word puzzle, all three ladies make a sport out of eye rolling. "Which means you should be able to look at the board, the players, and anticipate their moves. Or even their next five moves. All you have to do is outmaneuver him, just like you would a chess opponent."

Ding, ding, ding.

A light switches on in my brain. "While he's playing checkers, we'll play chess."

All three ladies, who've bonded far too quickly in my opinion, clap for real this time.

"All right, all right. Knock it off," I grouse.

Truth is, not only are they right, they're brilliant.

Now, I just have to hope I can beat my father at his power-trip game. It won't be as easy as one might think. After all, who do you think taught me how to play chess to begin with?

CHAPTER SIXTEEN

We work all week on the IPO and the upcoming new product launch like demons. Kendall has spent every night with me. It's been amazing to make love to her before we go to sleep, then wake up to her soft body molding into mine. We've settled into a comfortable routine, getting up every morning so we can shower together, have coffee and breakfast together, then ride to work together.

By the time the weekend rolls around, most of the work for the upcoming public stock issue is done, we're dead-ass tired, and we can use some rest and relaxation. As I load our luggage into the trunk of my Tesla, I wish I could tell Pink this was going to be a fun weekend getaway.

That would be a lie.

I still don't know what my father is up to, and the worry has my stomach churning.

Dex and Leo's only concern with my relationship with Kendall is that she's still my assistant. Even with a signed non-disclosure agreement, I have power over her, which is a bad idea. Some could argue it's irresponsible of me.

They'd be right, but now isn't the time to help her find a new job.

With her life in flux because of her niece's hearing problems, the custody case, and starting work at Checkmate, I'm willing to give it a little more time. At Oscar Wilde's she'd said she needed job stability, and I trust and care enough about Pink to give her what she's asking for until she's in a better personal place to make the transition to a new company.

When the time is right, I'll tell her she needs to move on. With my connections and her skills, she'll likely end up with a comparable salary, if not better. Especially with the recommendation she'll get from Checkmate.

Truth is I'm going to miss the hell out of having her with me all day.

I swerve around a city bus that's chugging along as I head to the Queens Midtown Tunnel to get to Long Island. My hand is on her bare thigh. It's Saturday morning, and Pink's breezy floral print dress that hits her mid-thigh and a pair of strappy, high-heeled sandals are perfect for a summer weekend in the Hamptons. I can't help but want the feel of her silky skin under my fingertips.

Myself, I'm wearing a pair of plaid shorts, a white linen shirt that's cuffed up at the sleeves, and a pair of prescription Ray-Ban shades. "I was thinking..." My fingers move in a circle against the inside of her thigh.

When my words trail off, she turns those chic pink-mirrored sunglasses on me and pretends to tap her knuckles against my head. "You? The biochemical genius thinking? I'm stunned."

I laugh. "Seriously," I say, glancing at her. Her hair is a tumble of messy curls that are bundled into a loose ponytail, and it drapes over one of her shoulders. "Jesus," I whisper. "You're so damn gorgeous."

She blushes. "That's the serious thing that's got you thinking?"

"Naw." I shake my head. "Being able to look at you is just a bonus." My fingers slip under the hem of her dress, still circling and massaging her sensitive flesh.

She hisses in a breath. "I don't want to smell like walking sex when we get to your parents' house." She uses Leo's description of us when we showed up at his apartment door after hours between my eighteen hundred thread count Egyptian cotton sheets.

I smile, tapping the brakes as we reach the tunnel. "I got us a room at a quaint inn. We can shower before we go to my parents'." Since Leo and Dex and their better halves are meeting us in the Hamptons, I got them a room at the same inn. I didn't tell my parents that my partners are attending the party. I figured the element of surprise would give me an advantage. That was Dad's strategy at the board meeting, so turnabout is fair play.

Pink covers my hand with hers, stopping my ascent. "I'm serious. I'm nervous enough after the way I met your father. It wasn't what I'd call an ideal first impression."

For the first time, I realize how nerve-racking this must be for her. This past week, we spent every evening talking over dinner and a bottle of wine about our histories. Now she knows I grew up with wealth and privilege, but she doesn't group me into the same category as her niece's baby daddy. The dickhead.

I guess I've been wallowing in the comfort and contentment of having her in my life and in my home. It's so easy between us. Selfishly, I hadn't thought much about how disturbing it must be for her to walk into an unfamiliar world after my father caught us in such a compromising position.

"I'm sorry." I squeeze her leg. "Would you rather I take you back to the city? I can do this alone."

She lifts a hand to my wavy hair and brushes it off my forehead. "Of course not. I've got your back."

Warmth floods my chest and makes my heart skip a beat.

"So, what were you thinking?" she asks.

"I was thinking you should consider moving in with me." I keep my focus on the road. Morning sun fills the car and washes over us. "Permanently."

Silence descends over the car.

I've made a mistake. Moved too fast. I'm about to retract my offer and apologize when Pink beats me to it.

"Are you sure?" she asks. "Because we're already skating on

thin ice at work. People are talking. Mamma Bear Leticia is trying to keep tongues from wagging, but eyebrows lift and everyone goes quiet when I walk into a room. You, your partners, and Leticia are the only Checkmate employees not gossiping about us."

Which is why office relationships are risky, even with a signed form of consent. I've never been involved with an employee, and I'd never use my position to manipulate a woman. I trust Pink not to slap me with an undeserving accusation of sexual misconduct, but the blowback at the office is obviously directed more at her because she's a woman.

Jesus, people and their double standards suck.

Precisely why there's a #metoo movement to begin with.

Maybe I suck harder. She's suffering at work because of me.

"I'm sure I want you to move in with me, but if you're not, I totally get it. No hard feelings." Just disappointment that runs deep.

"Maybe it's time I start looking for another job," she says sadly. "That would solve the problem, wouldn't it?"

My lips part. Leave it to Pink to assess the situation and be the brave one to step up with a solution that I've been tiptoeing around. With her work experience, I assumed she'd move on eventually, but she was the one who said she needed to stay at Checkmate until her niece's procedure is done and paid for.

"Yes, it would solve the problem. But..." *I'll miss seeing you during the day.*

Wow, I'm a sap.

"But you need help with the IPO." She finishes my sentence.

"That's not what I was going to say." Hell yes, we definitely need her help. "I was going to say you need the income."

She nods and sighs. "That's the problem. I'm getting paid by the same man I'm sleeping with. It looks bad for me."

"Then quit." If I have to choose between seeing Pink all day or having her share my home and my bed every night, I'll pick the latter any damn day of the week. "Move in with me and let me take care of your niece. Let me take care of *you* until you find another job."

Pink is already shaking her head.

I already think as highly of Pink as I do my partners, but my respect for her soars even more. Pink has distinct lines she won't cross for money or success. I love that about her, but this is different.

"I understood you not wanting to take my money when we first met, but things have definitely changed."

"I'd say," she teases.

"It isn't fair for you to quit a great paying job without a safety net, yet I don't want to wait to be an official couple until after you leave Checkmate and are job hunting." I accelerate around a Mercedes. "Quit and let me be your safety net."

"We can be an official couple without me moving in with you," she says.

"As long as you're living with another guy, it won't feel official to me," I counter.

"He's gay, remember?" she shoots back.

"I don't give a shit." I'm not backing down. "I take care of what's mine, so marry me."

I nearly swerve off the road.

What did I just fucking say?

Pink has gone as still as a stone statue.

For the first time in weeks, a weight lifts from my shoulders. My chest loosens. I don't remember ever being happier. I've spent long enough licking the wounds my ex-wife inflicted. It's time to move on, and I want to move on with this incredible woman sitting next to me.

No one else but her.

I lift her hand to my lips and feather soft kisses along the inside of her wrist while keeping my eyes on the road. "I love you, Pink, so whaddaya say?"

She hesitates, then finally says, "I'm not saying no..." Her voice is a whisper.

"But you're not saying yes?" I finish her sentence this time, pain pricking at my heart.

"It's just that...it's just that I've never let anyone take care of me." She stares straight ahead.

We're outside of the city now, and the scenery is transitioning from cement highways and honking horns to green grass, lush trees, and small town charm.

"I've never let myself trust anyone since my divorce, until I met you. Let's take a chance. Roll the dice. Hedge our bets on each other." My heart thuds in a sick rhythm. "Unless you don't love me." I don't care for a replay of my first marriage.

"I do love you." The words slip through her lips, so soft and sweet, and they're beautiful to my ears. "Lord, help me, but I do. It's the first time I've ever really been in love."

I let out a breath I didn't even realize I was holding. "Me, too." How ironic are those words?

"But you were married?" Her brow wrinkles.

"Yes," I say slowly, choosing my words carefully. "I would call it more like puppy love. I told you we were young. Too young, and we were both in it for the wrong reasons." She was in it for my trust fund. I was in it to make my parents happy. "This time it's different. You're different, and I'm different because of you."

Pink studies my profile for a long time. Then she pulls out her phone and types. "Done." Her phone let's out a swoosh, sending whatever she just typed zinging through cyberspace. "I quit." She drops her phone into her purse. "My resignation is waiting in your inbox." She leans over and sinks her teeth into my earlobe.

I mean she really *bites* me.

"Ouch." I flinch. "What was that for?" Not exactly the response I expected from the woman who just agreed to marry me.

"I'm a kept woman now," she says sternly. "Who has obligations to my niece. After my sister ended up trusting the wrong asshole, my parents warned me to never get myself into the same situation. I've already had sex with you more than once without a condom, and we've been so busy at work that I haven't made it to the doctor yet to get birth control." She suckles the spot that still stings from her teeth. Then she says with the most sexy, sultry tone I've ever heard, "If you hurt me, Oscar Strong, I will cut off your balls and mount them on my wall."

Then she puts her sunglasses on the dash, unbuckles her seatbelt, leans over the console, unzipping my shorts.

"Jesus, Pink." I white-knuckle the steering wheel with both hands when I realize she's about to go down on me. "I love your boldness and confidence, but it might get us killed."

Her mouth closes around my cock and she sucks. Hard.

A guy's gotta die somehow. When my number's up, I can't think of a better way to go than this. "Holy shit," I hiss out, trying to keep the car on the road.

Her ponytail falls across my lap, tickling my skin as her head bobs. She takes me so far in, I swear I practically hit the back of her throat.

While she's sucking my cock, she looks up at me. I glance down, and it's all I can do not to slam on the brakes. My vision blurs as she licks me from tip to root, then circles the head with her tongue. She plunges down on me again, filling her warm mouth with my pulsing dick.

"Goddamn, Pink, that's so good." My voice is so ragged, I sound like I'm in pain.

She sucks and bobs and sucks and bobs.

Fire shoots through me, lighting my nerve endings up like fireworks.

Truth is, her mouth, tongue, and lips working my granite-hard cock is pure bliss and pure torture at the same time. I grit my teeth and lean my head back against the headrest, forcing my eyes to stay open while she pumps my cock with her supple mouth. The noises she makes are pure heaven on Earth. My skin is searing with heat because I'm so turned on.

The first ache of orgasm tightens my balls. Every muscle I possess tightens and tenses, and I sink one set of fingers into the hair at the back of her head.

"That mouth of yours is made for my cock." My voice is a lusty growl.

That drives her on, and she increases her speed. Adds pressure. Keeps fucking me with that incredible mouth.

"Pink," I growl, wrapping her ponytail around my hand to pull her off me so I won't come in her mouth.

She resists, sucking harder and flicking her tongue along my length.

I explode in her mouth, and she swallows me down.

I'm panting and trying to keep my attention on the road with the last of my orgasm pumping into her lovely mouth.

When she's done, she zips my shorts and buckles her seatbelt.

"Good God, woman. You're amazing," I say, taking her hand.

She shoots me a heart-stopping smile. "I know." She puts on her sunglasses and slides them up the bridge of her nose.

"I'd tell you to dial down your enthusiasm, but then my life would become infinitely less exciting." I laugh. When we get to the inn, I'm going to fuck her until the windows rattle from her shouts of pleasure.

Yes, this woman I love is going to make my life much, much more interesting.

CHAPTER SEVENTEEN

I do exactly what I promised myself I'd do once we arrive at the inn in East Hampton. I bend Pink over the bed and take her from behind so we can both enjoy the stunning view of the ocean, which our room offers because of the huge windows and sliding glass doors. She climaxes twice, clutching the plush down comforter in both hands while the ocean just outside our room laps against the white sandy beach. Then we move to the antique-style footed bathtub and do it all over again.

I'm not usually a bath taking kind of guy, but Pink loves the tub, so I take it for a spin with Pink riding me so hard that water splashes over the sides onto the seafoam green marble floor.

By the time we're dressed and ready to go to my parents', Dex sends me a text to let me know he, Ava, Leo, and Chloe have checked in, too.

Mills House Inn is one of the finest boutique hotels in the world, yet it's quaint. I wanted the weekend to be special for Pink, at least the time when we're alone.

I doubt *special* is the word I'd use to describe the time we'll spend at my parents' cottage later today.

I text Leo and Dex to let them know we'll meet them in ten minutes in the great room—the inn's version of a lobby.

Pink is leaning close to the full-length mirror, applying shimmery lip gloss, so I trek toward her. She's dressed in an elegant linen sundress fit for a garden party. Of course, it's a light shade of pink. Her hair is swept up into a stylish knot at the base of her head, and loose curls tumble around her face. The finishing touch is a pair of large, gold hoop earrings, and the classic string of pearls she wore the first time I met her.

"You're beautiful." I thread my arms around her waist and look over her shoulder.

Our gazes lock as we stare at each other in the mirror.

She rubs her glossy lips together, then leans back against me.

"You make me feel beautiful, Oscar," she says softly. The sound of my real name on her lips is even more exciting than when she screams my nickname while we're making love. She covers my hands with one of hers, and I place a gentle kiss at her temple, swaying gently back and forth with her in my arms. "The way you look at me. The way you touch me." One side of her pouty lips lift. "The way you fuck me."

I sink my teeth into the cusp of her ear. Not as firmly as she did mine in the car, but just enough for the sweet sting to tell her I mean business. "If you keep talking dirty, we'll never make it to my parents' house."

She laughs. "One f-bomb is all it takes to turn you on?"

"With you? Damn straight," I say, swatting her rump.

"Do that again later?" she teases.

Just the thought makes my dick harden like a plank of wood.

"Absolutely." I tug her toward the door.

"On second thought, maybe we better not get too rough." Her hand drops to her tummy.

My eyes fly wide. "You're...you're....?" I smile so big I can feel it to my bones.

"I don't know." She hurries to explain. "It's way too soon to tell. I'm only a few days late, so it's probably nothing."

"It's not nothing, Pink. It's...it's..."

She holds her breath, waiting for me to finish.

"It's fantastic," I say. I mean it. I really do.

She lets out a long, slow breath, her eyes sliding shut. "I wasn't going to tell you until I knew for sure, but then you proposed in the car, and then..." She blushes, and it melts my heart.

"Then you gave me the best blow job of my life?" I finish her sentence.

"Really? It was the best?" Her teasing look tells me she's busting my balls.

"Yes." I take her chin between my thumb and finger. "And don't you ever unbuckle your seatbelt and put yourself and our child in danger like that again."

"Potential child," she corrects, stepping away to snatch her purse off the wingback chair. "What should we say to your friends and your parents?" Her expression turns more serious. Solemn.

"About us getting hitched?" I stop and tug her against me. "Or about..." I nod to her belly.

She shakes her head. "Keep my uterus between us for now. I meant about us getting engaged. This is..." She glances around the six hundred dollar a night suite. "It's incredibly romantic, and the Hamptons are magical." She slings the dainty, long-strapped purse over a shoulder. "This is the first time I've ever been here, but this party your parents are throwing doesn't sound like it's going to be much fun for you and your partners. It's not how I envisioned announcing my engagement. I'm not sure I've envisioned anything, really. It happened so fast."

I lace my arms around her waist once again. "I think we should wait until we go shopping for a ring." I plan to put a diamond the size of Delaware on her finger. "We'll buy it as soon as we get back to the city tomorrow evening." I place an open-mouthed kiss in the nook of her neck. "You're the event planner. How about you put together a party at my place..." I stumble over the word. Then a wide smile spreads across my face until my cheeks ache. "Put together a party at *our* place for next weekend. We'll announce it then. I'll break the news about your separation from the company to Leo and Dex Monday morning and have Leticia start looking for a replacement."

We've got enough on our plates, dealing with my dad in a few minutes without adding in our change in relationship status. I at least want Pink to enjoy our night in this gorgeous room, and I want picking out a ring tomorrow evening to be a sentimental experience she'll never forget.

One she can tell our kids and grandkids.

The thought steals my breath, and I know that I can handle whatever it is my dad is about to lob at me—as long as Pink is at my side.

My partners may piss and moan about me losing another assistant, but they'll understand, even though it leaves us short-handed again. Leticia, on the other hand, will likely castrate me.

Bright side, the company no longer has to worry about me being romantically involved with my assistant.

Pink adjusts the collar of my shirt, then molds both palms against my chest. "When you talk to Dex and Leo about me quitting, tell them they've got some great options."

"Like?" I love her sharp mind. She's already thinking about solutions.

"You could hire another overqualified assistant who is a self-starter, like me. Or you could bring in an army of temps." She's confident enough in herself to know that she and Leticia both do the work of a dozen employees. "Or I can work from home next week. No one will know I'm doing the work, and I won't have to face the employee gossip mill. No wagging tongues. No lifting eyebrows." She toys with my top button. "And you'll be getting a damn good employee for free now that I've resigned."

I let out a low, naughty chuckle. "I guarantee I'll figure out another means of compensation. And my tongue is the only one that will be wagging when I taste you every night."

"You're a horn-dog, you know that?" She pinches my shoulder.

I tilt my head to one side. "I do know that. Good news is I'm only that way with you." My tone turns serious. "From the moment

I first saw you in my waiting room, you've been the only one for me."

"Then let's do this thing." She mimics what she said to me in the board meeting when I was rattled by my father's unexpected appearance. "Together."

On the way to the great room, Leo texts that they are already waiting in the parking lot, so I detour and go straight outside. Dex and Ava are already in the back seat of a Bentley SUV. Leo is helping Chloe into the front passenger side. "'Bout time," Leo says.

"When did you get this thing?" I gawk at the midnight blue metallic paint shimmering under the afternoon sky.

"The old ball and chain made me trade my sports car for a family vehicle." Leo shoots me a look that says he'd rather have had a root canal than let go of his sports car, but then he winks.

Chloe rolls her eyes so far back in her head I can see the whites of her eyes. "I wanted a van—"

Leo hurries to shut her door. "I am not driving a minivan." He jogs around to the driver's side.

"This is your idea of a family car?" I deadpan as Leo opens his door. "This is a six liter, twin turbo that does zero to one hundred in four seconds. I've seen Lamborghinis on the Autobahn with less horsepower."

With one foot in the car, he shrugs. "I won't go over the speed limit when the baby is with me. At least I still have my man card, though." He disappears inside his new family Batmobile.

The guy has a point.

I laugh and shake my head, opening the passenger door of my Tesla for Pink. As I walk around to the driver's side, I try to picture myself getting into a minivan. I gotta be honest. It doesn't really seem like my jam.

The engine roars to life. "Please tell me I don't have to trade this baby for a minivan." I stroke the steering wheel lovingly.

Pink tips her chin to stare at me over the rim of her glasses.

"How about a Tesla SUV?" I bargain for my own man card the way Leo obviously did.

Pink slides her glasses back up on her nose. "Will you put a baby on board sign on the window?"

I throw my head back and laugh. "For you and our kid, I'll put one on every window."

We rumble out of the parking lot, and Leo falls in behind us. Life is good.

Except for the fact that I'm going to meet with my father, and I know it's going to ruin my whole goddamn day. I only hope that whatever he's got planned doesn't ruin my entire life.

CHAPTER EIGHTEEN

We turn into the circular drive of my parents' place, and Pink grabs my arm.

"*This* is a cottage?" Her nails dig into my arm. She's clutching the oh shit bar with her other hand, and she's breathing so hard I'm afraid she's about to hyperventilate. "You said your parents were rich, but *this?*"

I pull through the drive and stop in front of the valet. Then I roll down my window. "I'm family," I tell the young man. "I'll pull into the private drive along the side of the estate." I hook a finger over my shoulder. "The car behind me will do the same."

He nods.

I roll up my window and follow the path that will allow me to park out of sight of the general crowd that's attending Mom and Dad's *get-together.* I knew there'd be enough people here to fill a cruise ship.

I park in the shade and kill the engine. "You sure you want to do this?" I ask Pink. "Because you don't have to."

"I used to watch *Love Story* with my mom when I was growing up. It was her favorite movie of all time. Now I know how Ali MacGraw's character felt when she had to meet her fiancé's parents." Pink turns to me. "You're a lot like Ryan O'Neal's character. You're so...so...not *this*. It's hard to believe you come from this world."

It's the best compliment I could ask for. "Thank you."

Pink leans forward and looks up through the windshield at the sprawling mansion. "How many square feet is this place?"

I shrug with a wrist dangling over the steering wheel. "Seven thousand. Give or take."

When she tucks a strand of hair behind her ear, her hand tremors slightly, so I don't tell her this used to be just our weekend and summer house. It wasn't until a few years ago that my parents sold our main estate in New Rochelle, which was twice as grand, and moved to the cottage full time.

Her hand goes to her mouth, as though she's going to be sick.

"Kendall." I take her hand between both of mine. "You're not alone. I'm here." I hitch my chin toward the back of the car, where Leo is pulling up behind us. "They're here. It's going to be fine, but I don't want you to do anything you don't feel comfortable with."

Frankly, if I were in her shoes, I wouldn't feel any more uncomfortable if I were getting a prostate exam. Plus, Pink's strappy, high-heeled shoes would pinch me like a motherfucker. Sexy as they are, they make me glad I was born a dude. Even happier that I'm not a drag queen. Those guys are my heroes to wear the shit they do like naturals.

She draws in a deep breath, as though that steadies her nerves. "I can do this."

I study her, then I finally say, "Okay." I hand her my keys. "Can you put these in your purse? I don't want to be tempted to ram my car into the side of the house if my dad pisses me off. Or use them as a weapon if my half-brother shows up."

Pink's lips part.

"I'm joking." Not really, but she's already worried, and I don't want to make it worse.

She takes my keys and drops them into her shoulder bag.

We all climb out of both cars.

Dex whistles. "Holy shit, Oz. I knew you grew up with money, but this is almost scary."

We've known each other for years, but there's a reason I never brought my partners to my parents' home. Leo and Dex didn't grow up with money, and it's intimidating as hell. If my dad wasn't blackmailing me, I wouldn't be subjecting them or Pink to any of this now.

"Thanks." I walk over and fist bump both of my partners. "I appreciate you both being here. I'm sorry it's come to this."

Dex says, "From the beginning, when we were still chess team geeks, it's always been one for all—"

"And all for one," Leo finishes.

Our three ladies join us. A sense of contentment that I've never experienced fills me.

I look up into the blue sky. White pillowy clouds are scooting along on the warm summer breeze. "You all are my family. You know that, right?"

"I'm only here for the free champagne," Dex says with a half-cocked grin.

Leo shrugs. "I only came hoping to bump into Alec Baldwin. He's from East Hampton, right? I never miss an SNL episode when he's hosting."

I love these guys, especially when they're busting my chops.

We follow the garden path that's alight with vibrant, blooming flowers in different shades of purples, reds, and oranges. Wisteria winds up a trellis and covers the arch over our heads as we step into the clearing, the back lawn sprawling in front of us with the ocean in the distance.

No question, it's a beautiful place with a breathtaking view. Unfortunately, not much to offer once you scratch beneath the surface. If I learned nothing else from my first marriage, it's that a real home isn't defined by its grandeur. It's the people inside and their hearts that turn a house into a refuge.

Give me a brownstone in the city over this any day. Or give me a middle class American home with a picket fence, which is what

I'm sure Pink grew up in after meeting her family. It beats the hell out of a mansion with no concept of unconditional love from the people who own it.

As we stroll across the lawn toward the crowd, a string quartet plays under the gazebo.

I spot my father schmoozing the attendees of his *get-together*, which number in the hundreds. He's wearing a nautical jacket—his version of casual.

I lace my fingers with Pink's, draw in a deep breath, and walk in the direction of the bar. A little liquor never hurts at a time like this.

We mingle through the crowd, trying to make our way to the open bar that's set up next to the Olympic-size swimming pool. From the corner of my eye, I see my father glance in our direction, then do a double take. He's seen us, but I'm going to play it cool and hard to get.

After all, one of the rules of chess is to never let your opponent see fear. I made that mistake in the board meeting. I won't make it again.

We step up to the bar, and I take the liberty of ordering my partners' favorites. Ava asks for a wine spritzer, and Chloe orders sparkling water.

"Sparkling water for me, as well," says Pink with a nervous smile. Her hand grazes her tummy for the briefest of moments.

Chloe's eyes fly wide. Of course, she'd be the one to figure out our secret so easily.

I widen mine, too, as a warning for Chloe to keep quiet.

Luckily, my partners are too obtuse to catch on, and Ava doesn't seem to notice either.

I pretend not to notice that my dad is making his way toward us.

"I see you've brought the cavalry with you, son," Dad says, infiltrating our circle. He shakes hands with Leo and Dex, giving a nod to the ladies. When he looks at Pink, he gives her a pasty smile and stiffens.

"Sweetheart!" Mom walks up, too. It's the first time I've seen her in months, and I've got to say, I've missed her. She's not a bad person or a bad mother. She's just never been strong enough to risk standing up to my father, so she's always played along with his games.

"Mom." I kiss her on the cheek and give her a big hug.

She's holding what looks like a mimosa in a champagne glass, a Checkmate bracelet from the fashion show and brunch dangling from her wrist.

"Nice." I finger the gold knight chess piece medallion. "Kendall had these made." I nod to my girl.

"Oh," Mom says, her eyes widening. "Hello." She's at least trying to appear hospitable. "Your father said you might be bringing someone." She turns to Kendall. "Lovely to meet you."

"Mom, you know Leo and Dex." She greets them, then I introduce her to Ava and Chloe.

"Oh, heavens, you must be pretty far along," Mom says, staring at Chloe's belly. The ladies break off to talk birthing rooms and something called Braxton Hicks and Kegels.

I do not want to know.

Dad stuffs a hand in his pants pocket and rocks back on his heels. "Let's go to my study and chat, shall we."

Wow. That didn't take long. The pleasantries have been swiftly dispensed, and Dad wants to get right to it.

"After you." I point toward the house.

When Dex and Leo fall in behind me, Dad stops. "This is a father-son talk. I'll return him shortly. You boys eat, drink, and be merry while we're gone." Dad strolls toward the glass French doors that lead into the house.

"I'll be fine, but if you happen to see a mushroom cloud go up over the house, you know I've lost my temper and you should seek shelter for the ladies." I blow out an irritated breath and follow my dad.

Once we're in Dad's office, I so badly want to say, "J. Paul Getty called and wants his office back", but I don't. The dark brown leather furniture, mahogany desk, and hunter green walls make a statement that shouts old money and power.

"Bringing your partners to intimidate me was a dirty trick." Dad sets his glass of scotch down on the desk and sinks into his executive chair. The rich supple leather squeaks under his weight.

"Not as dirty as hijacking my board meeting and holding my company for ransom."

"I have to say, that's a great comeback." He points to one of the armchairs across from his desk. "Have a seat, son."

"I'll stand, thanks. At least until you tell me why I'm here, and why you're screwing with my company and my future."

He picks up his scotch. "Aha." His index finger lifts from the glass and he points at me, then takes a long drink. "Our future is exactly the point. We want you to spend more time with us. Be a real family, like when you were younger."

"I'm not eight anymore, Dad."

He swirls the scotch around in the expensive crystal glass I remember him having shipped in from Europe. "It's time to settle down, don't you think? Maybe give us a few grandchildren." He said as much in my lab.

I can't help but wonder where he's going with it. "Workin' on it."

Dad frowns. "You know your mother and I hate it when you speak like white trash."

Which is why I do it. "I speak like an average American guy. What's wrong with that?"

"You're not average. Not in any way." Dad lets out an exasperated breath. "That's what's wrong with it."

I shrug. "Doesn't change my answer. I'm workin' on it."

He gives me a sly smile, lifting a finger in the direction of the back lawn. "Come on. You can do better than the girl you were screwing in the closet."

My anger spikes. I feel that mushroom cloud I warned my partners about coming on, and I clamp both hands to my sides so I don't shred this place to its foundations. With my bare hands.

"First, don't talk about Kendall, or I swear to God I'll never speak to you again." My voice is low and lethal. Frankly, my father is lucky I don't climb over his desk and teach him some manners. "Second, I let you pick my first wife from a list of pedigreed names that met your approval. Jill may've been from an upper-crust family, but she acted like trash. I could pull a hooker off the street in Harlem who'd likely have more class than Jill did. And the hooker would have slept around a lot less to boot, so no damn way am I going down that road with you again. I've made my choice and it's Kendall."

His brows bunch. "You're going to marry her?" he says with a scoff. "You and your brother." Dad shakes his head. "At least you didn't pick a drug addict like he did."

"Speaking of acting like white trash, where is Grant?"

Dad glowers. "He'll be here shortly, and don't talk about my son with such disrespect."

And the two percent wonders why they're hated.

I don't know what's more astonishing—the fact that Dad doesn't recognize his own snobbery for what it is, or his double standards.

"What's done is done." Dad sighs into his glass, then drinks. "Your mother and I are going to set your brother's mistake right."

Must be talking about Grant being a father soon. I feel sorry for the poor kid, and it's not even born yet. I wouldn't wish that douche, Grant, on anyone. "In my lab, you said Grant wasn't getting married. How do you intend to 'fix his mistake'?"

The way Dad purses his lips makes something prickle down my spine. "Please tell me you're not going to try to pay the girl off so she'll have an abortion?"

"Of course not," Dad huffs. But then he can't hold my gaze, and I know he's probably done much worse.

"If she's not having an abortion, and Grant isn't marrying her, then what?" I ask. Honestly, I'd rather not know, but my dickhead half-brother is somehow intertwined with my father's desperate grasp for power over me.

"The child is going to live with us."

I sputter with laughter. "You're going to raise Grant's baby?"

"Don't be a smartass," Dad barks. "Grant is moving in with us, too, so he can help raise her."

Must've had a sonogram if they already know the gender. "I'm guessing you've offered the mother—unlucky lady that she is—a fortune to support her drug habit if she's willing to give up her child to Grant."

"Grant is going to step up and do the right thing."

Dad's guilt over leaving Grant's mom to run off with my mother still runs deep if he can continue to defend a douche like my half-brother.

"Okay, we've covered the bases of Grant's sorry existence." I cross my arms. "What does this have to do with me and my company?"

"We need to present a united front." He parrots the same phrase he used in my lab. "Create a happy family atmosphere. It will look good for the custody hearing."

The *what?*

Obviously, the mother isn't handing over her kid willingly. Thank God. "No judge in their right mind will give Grant custody of a kid." I snort.

"They will if you testify on his behalf as a character witness. The owners of Checkmate have weathered a few storms and built a solid reputation." There it is. Dad's bottom line. "If you can find a suitable wife, even better."

My mouth turns sour at that word. Suitable is exactly how he described Jill when he was rushing me into an engagement and then down the aisle before I could change my mind.

"We'd like more grandchildren so Grant's daughter will grow up with cousins. When you get married again, you and your family could have the east wing of the cottage. It'll be the picture of family unity that any court will drool over."

Jesus fucking Christ.

"You're using my company as leverage to get me to spend more time with you and lie under oath for Grant? You think that will make for happy family dinners every night?" I pinch my lips together. "Maybe we'll hold hands around the dinner table and say grace after you've threatened all I've worked for and everything I've *earned* on my own? After you've made me lie for an asswipe like Grant? *And* after trying to push me into another marriage I don't want?" I blow out a breath. I just can't believe my damn ears.

Dad shrugs. "There's an array of eligible young women out there dying to meet you. Any one of them would love to live in a house like this."

Fire burns in my stomach, rising up to singe the back of my throat.

"Why'd you ask me to bring Pink?" I say through gritted teeth.

"Pink?" Dad frowns.

I draw in a breath at my mistake. I'm so damn mad, I didn't think to use her real name. "It's a nickname."

"A nickname like that should tell you something, for God's sake." Dad slams his glass down on the desk. "I wanted to prove to you how unsuitable she really is. That's why I invited you to bring her, and you just proved my point."

What a bastard. "You wanted to humiliate her?" I blow out a low laugh and shake my head. "It never occurred to you that she's a nice person who doesn't deserve to be humiliated, and hurting her means you hurt me."

"You're missing the point entirely," Dad roars. "Once we win the custody battle for Grant's daughter, she'll be in better hands with us than with that drug-addicted little twit she has for a mother. She's already got enough problems since she's losing her hearing. She'll need to adjust to the cochlear implants once the procedure is done, and we want to create a family environment so she'll know she's better off here than in some trailer park upstate."

I freeze, letting my whirring brain catch up to the reality of the situation.

"Did you just say...?" Surely, I didn't hear him correctly. I'd assumed when Dad said he and Mom were going to be grandparents, he'd meant Grant's baby was on the way. But...

"Oh, my God," I whisper in disbelief. "It's you. You're the scum trying to take Avery's daughter away. She came to you for help, and you're screwing her over." I take a step back.

"You know the girl's mother?"

"You son of a bitch." I turn and stalk out of his office to go find Pink before my mother has one too many mimosas and lets on that the Randolph clan are the monsters trying to destroy Kendall's family.

"I'll take over your company and push you out," Dad calls after me.

I don't stop walking toward the back door. "You can try," I say over a shoulder. "But I'll fight you to my dying breath." This time I do stop. "For the record, Avery and her daughter don't live in a trailer park." I storm out without waiting for another retort from my father.

There is no way in hell I'm letting my parents take a little girl from her loving family just because they don't have enough money to fight a financial giant. And I'll never give up fighting for Checkmate either.

CHAPTER NINETEEN

I crash through the French doors that soar to the ceiling, and beeline it toward Pink, hoping to whisk her away so I can break the awful news to her. I want to be the one to tell her that my half-brother is the douche who was too much of a wuss to do right by her sister and niece. That my parents are the monsters trying to destroy her family.

She deserves to hear it from me.

She's standing by the gazebo with my mom, Ava, and Chloe. Dex and Leo are standing about twenty feet away and have been commandeered by a few of our investors who've shown up to the party.

No surprise that my father invited them as a show of his influence over our board.

I detour and say to my partners as I pass, "We're done here. Let's go." I ignore our investors. I don't know what my father has on them or what favors he's called in, but those pussies are out as far as I'm concerned. We'll either find new investors or we'll open our stock to the general public first, without these douches anteing up from their deep pockets. That will put Checkmate at risk because the point of putting together the list of heavy hitting investors we have now is to make sure the stock is snatched up immediately, which will make the value soar. Opening it up to the general public with no lineup of investors as a safety net could make the stock drop.

Jesus, it sucks to be me. What sucks even harder is that I haven't just fucked up my life. I'm also fucking up the lives of the people I care about most in the world—Dex, Leo, and Pink.

Dex and Leo break off from the group and follow me. Just as I'm about to reach Pink, I'm practically clotheslined, and I don't see it coming.

"Hey, little brother," Grant says, and hooks an arm around my neck.

"Get away from me, you bastard." My voice couldn't be any more lethal if it were a nine-millimeter bullet fired at point-blank range.

"Whoa." Grant lets me go, and I realize he's got the same light blond hair as Pink's niece. "Who pissed in your Cheerios?"

How original. No one has ever accused Grant of being intelligent. A smartass, yes. A dumbass, *hell* yes. But intelligent? Not a chance in hell. "You did. Now get the hell away from me."

The ruckus draws attention from my mom, and her look says she's afraid we're going to cause a scene in front of her guests.

Too damn bad. Should've thought of that before making a play to steal a kid who belongs to someone else.

"Calm down, Oscar," Dad says, walking up behind me.

I spin around. "Calm down?" I'm seething. "Are you fucking kidding me?"

"Come now, boys." Mom hurries over. "Don't embarrass your father in front of his friends."

Grant kisses my mom on the cheek, as though nothing's going on. "Sorry I'm late, Mom." He calls her mom to make my father happy, ensuring that the money will keep rolling into his bank account.

"Oh, my God," I hear Pink gasp.

My eyes slide shut. I don't want to turn around and look at her because I know what I'm going to see.

"*You.*" Her voice is laced with pain, betrayal, and disbelief.

I swallow the dread bubbling up to burn my throat, and I turn to face her. She's staring wide-eyed at Grant.

Fuck me.

"You're...you're the jerk who got my sister pregnant and left her flat." Pink's voice is thready and she's pale. "I met you at the diner when you were dating my sister. It's where she met you, and you'd come in to see her...you'd come to pick her up at the end of her shifts."

Grant blanches. "I have no idea what she's talking about," he says to no one in particular.

Way to go, big brother. Still incapable of acting like a man and taking responsibility for yourself.

"You're the drug addict's sister?" my dad asks, just as stunned as Pink.

"My sister is *not* a drug addict." Pink's angry tone matches her expression.

I go to stand by her. "Pink, I didn't—"

She holds up a hand and backs away. "Don't come near me. You lied. Is your last name even Strong? Because theirs..." She turns fiery eyes on my parents and then Grant. "Your last name is Randolph. The papers you had served to my sister says so."

"I...I changed my name years ago," I say, and take a step toward her. If I could just touch her. Hold her. She'll know how sorry I am about all of this.

But she backs farther away to stay out of my reach. "You forgot to mention that." It's not a question. "How convenient."

Hell, I never tell anyone my last name used to be Randolph. It's been so long that I never think about it myself. It's something I'd rather forget.

The guests have gone quiet, and no one moves, as though time has stopped and the Earth isn't rotating anymore.

"You're the little girl's aunt?" Mom asks.

"The little girl?" Pink lets out a disbelieving laugh. "You don't even know her name, do you? Or is it that you just don't care?" She throws her hands in the air, looking around with a wild look in her eye. "Stupid question. Of course you don't care. Your sorry excuse for a son—" She points at Grant. "—gets my sister pregnant, leaves her with no help whatsoever because *you two* didn't think she's good enough, and none of you bothered to so much as inquire about your own grandchild until recently."

My mother drops her champagne glass, looking weak in the knees. "Of course we know her name, but we didn't know she existed until your sister came to us for help." Mom shoots Grant a look that says he's been lying to them as much as he's lied to Pink's sister.

"And your way of helping was to sue for custody of a child you've never even met?" Pink is slowly backing away.

"Because her mother is a drug addict!" Dad roars.

"My sister has never done drugs a day in her life!" Pink shouts back.

"Dad." I'm clenching my fists so tight my nails dig into my palms. "Shut. Up."

Grant stays quiet like the douche he is.

Dear God. How am I related to these people? "We'll figure this out, Kendall, I promise. Let's just go."

"You expect me to believe anything you have to say now?" She turns her fury on me. "What kind of monsters are you people?" She takes another step back, and her gaze lands on Dex, then slides to Ava. A ragged breath slips through her parted lips. "Oh, my God. You *all* set me up. You sent your partner upstate to target me, didn't you? It couldn't have been a coincidence that Dex was in the diner and coaxed me into calling you for a job. And I fell for it." Pink frames her head with both hands. "I'm such an idiot. I thought you loved me. Thought you meant it when you asked me to marry you on the way here. Wow. You're good. You even got me to quit my job so you wouldn't have to fire me. So I couldn't sue you or even draw unemployment, because my resignation is already waiting in your inbox."

"Pink, no. That's not what—"

She stops breathing, a tear sliding from under her sunglasses to streak her beautiful cheek. The wetness shimmers under the afternoon sun.

I want to wrap her in my arms, kiss her tears away, and set her world right.

Instead, all I've done is make her world crumble.

She wraps her arms around her stomach. "You set my family up with an attorney who will help your parents win, didn't you?" Her hand splays over her belly, and I know she's thinking I'll do the same to her if it turns out she's carrying my child.

She turns and runs toward the parking lot.

"Pink!" I break into a run after her.

"Let her go," Grant speaks up for the first time. "Good riddance. She's trailer trash like her sister."

I stop cold in my tracks. "I'm going to kick your ass into the next century." I start for my half-brother.

The crowd gasps.

Chloe let's out a wail of pain and clutches her stomach as she bends forward. "Oh, God," she rasps. "I think my water just broke."

Leo, Ava, and Dex rush to Chloe's side.

I stand there grinding my teeth. It takes every ounce of willpower I have not to throttle Grant, my dad, and my mom all at the same time.

Chloe lets out another howl, and she braces her weight against Leo.

"I've got to get her to the hospital," Leo says.

"There's no time." Chloe is panting like she's run a marathon. "I think the baby's coming now."

The guests scatter.

I take out my phone. "I'm calling 911."

A mid-forties guy with a sweater tied around his neck, looking like he's ready to attend a tennis match at Wimbledon, steps forward. "I'm a doctor. Let's get her inside." In my experience, any guy with a sweater tied around his neck is probably a dick, but if he can help Chloe, then I'll keep my mouth shut.

I go to Dex and Ava. "Please be a buffer between my parents and Chloe while I go find Kendall." I don't wait for an answer. My keys are in Pink's purse, so I'm hoping she's waiting in the car. I don't walk, I run to the side of the estate where I parked.

But my car is gone. And so is the love of my life.

CHAPTER TWENTY

I stalk back to the house as sirens sound in the distance, cutting through the peaceful, summer afternoon breeze. They grow closer and louder by the time I walk into the main sitting room just inside the double French doors.

A painful shriek billows from a bedroom down the hall, where Chloe is waiting for the paramedics.

I run both sets of fingers through my hair. I think of Kendall in labor, having my child, and I don't want to be shut out of their lives. Not being able to share the sonogram, not hearing the baby's heartbeat. Not pressing my hand to Pink's stomach when our child kicks would shatter my world.

I'm nothing without her.

My dad, my mom, and Grant are huddled in the corner by the wet bar. I can't hear their conversation, but their body language tells me my parents are raking Grant over the coals for screwing them over the same way he screwed over Pink's sister.

'Bout time. My dad has enabled Grant for far too long, which is why my half-brother is such a dickhead. My mom has enabled my father even longer, which is why Dad still tries to buy his way through life.

Dex and Ava emerge from the hall as the blare of sirens pulls up out front.

I go open the door. "Ava, take them to Chloe."

Ava hustles back down the hallway with the paramedics on her heels. They're loaded with equipment and a stretcher.

"How's Kendall?" Dex asks.

"She left in my car." I scrub a hand down my face. "I'm sorry I fucked things up for our company. Unfortunately, I'm going to have to fuck them up even more if I want a chance at salvaging things with Kendall," I say to Dex. "I need you to trust me and be my wingman, even though Checkmate might take a hit. Can you do that?"

"'Course," Dex says without hesitation. Without question.

I notch my chin toward my family, who are still arguing by the wet bar. It damn well kills me to have to call them family, but whatever. I know who my real family is, and it has nothing to do with DNA or surnames.

Dex follows me.

"Honey," Mom says when I approach.

Dad says at the same time, "Son—"

I hold up a hand to shut them the hell up. "Don't even. All three of you sicken me."

I start with Grant first. "You are dead to me. I don't care if Kendall never forgives me. I'll still make sure you never have access to that little girl who has nothing in common with you beyond your sperm. If you ever bother Avery or Hannah again, I will hunt you down and personally make sure you can never sire another child." I give Grant a dismissive wave of my hand, as though he's no more important to me than something I'd scrape off the bottom of my shoe after walking in a dog park.

"And you two..." I turn my ire on my parents.

"We thought she was a drug addict," Mom whispers.

"I don't care." I'm gritting my teeth so hard, I swear I feel a tooth crack. "You didn't bother to find out for sure. You took *his* word for it." I nod at Grant, who's looking sullen. "If you'd bothered to get to know Avery instead of jumping to conclusions and offering to *buy her daughter*, you'd have figured out that she's a good kid."

My mom tears up, and my dad stares at his shoes, as though they're both ashamed.

"That's right. A kid. Who Grant lied to and took advantage of just because she works in a diner and lives in the wrong zip code. I've met her. Spent time with her, and she's not an addict. She's just a young, gullible woman, and she's been treated badly by this... this..." I can't think of a word vile enough to describe my half-brother.

"Oscar," Dex says in a low voice, obviously to calm me down so I don't cross a line.

"Coming through!" The paramedics wheel Chloe through the living room on a stretcher.

Dex and I jog over, and I clasp Leo on the shoulder as the paramedics maneuver the stretcher up the marble steps so they can get to the door. "It'll be okay, buddy," I say to my friend. My friend who is closer than my blood brother will ever be.

Ava's following close behind the paramedics. "I want to go to the hospital, Dex."

"Go," I say to Dex. "I've got this."

"You sure?" Dex's concern shows in his worried expression. "I don't want to get a call that you've been arrested for a violent crime."

I shake my head and glance at my parents and Grant. "I'll keep my cool. They aren't important enough anymore to give them that much power over me. I'll call you as soon as I'm done here."

When the paramedics are gone, I return to my parents. "Here's how it's gonna go down." I cross my arms over my chest so I don't put my fist through a wall. "You're going to step away from my company and drop this pathetic attempt to manipulate me by making a play for control of Checkmate."

My dad starts to speak, but I make sure to give him an acid glare that could melt solid steel.

"You're also going to drop the ridiculous custody suit and leave Avery, Hannah, and their entire family alone. If you don't, I will never speak to either of you again."

My mom starts to weep.

"And if you ever come close to doing something this low again when it comes to me or anyone I care about, I'll go to every business person you know, every country club or social organization you belong to, and tell them what you've tried to do to a little girl who is losing her hearing because her dipshit sperm donor wouldn't acknowledge his own child."

I mow both of my parents down with another hard stare. "You won't be able to join a bridge club when I'm done."

I hold out my hand and look at Grant. "Now give me the keys to your car. Because of you, the wonderful woman who I'd planned to marry has left me, and I need to find her."

Grant digs his keys out of his pocket and drops them into my palm. "It's the silver Jag."

I stroll toward the door without another word. With any luck, Pink will listen to me and allow me to make this right. Although, I wouldn't blame her if she never wanted to see me again.

I head straight for the valet, because no way in hell would Grant ever park his own car the way I did. Within minutes I'm sliding behind the wheel of Grant's Jag, and kicking up dust as I peel out of the drive. On my way out of the drive, I make sure to scrape the passenger side against the brick pillar that encases the mailbox.

Ooops. Sorry, not sorry.

I breathe a sigh of relief when I get to the inn, and my Tesla is parked in the lot. I run to our room, blowing through the door. My heart drops to my feet. Her bag is gone, and the keys to my car are laying in the middle of the bed. I go to the landline and dial the concierge.

"What can I do for you, Mr. Strong?" A chipper voice streams through the line.

What can you do for me? Oh, I don't know. Maybe do me a favor and put me out of my misery?

I rub my forehead.

"Do you happen to know where my fiancée..." My heart pinches when I think of how short-lived our engagement was. I suppose it happened too fast. We burned too hot and too bright only to fizzle out before our time. "Do you know where Ms. Tate went?"

The concierge hesitates, obviously because I don't know where my own fiancée has gone. "The inn's private driver took her back to the city, sir."

"How long has she been gone?" I ask, already gathering up my things so I can follow her.

"Fifteen minutes," the concierge says.

"Where was the driver taking her?" I bark. She's likely either going to one of three places—HQ to clean out her desk, my place to gather up all of her belongings, or to her friend's apartment, where she'd been staying before she all but moved in with me. I don't want to waste any time by having to check each place and hope I get it right.

"Well, sir...I'm not allowed to give out that infor—"

I slam down the phone, pick up my bag, and hurry to the great room. When I get to the concierge's desk, I lean over and say in a low, deadly voice so he knows I'm not fucking around, "I need to know the address where your driver is taking Ms. Tate."

The concierge's eyes round into saucers at my tone.

"I'm assuming this inn prefers excellent reviews from high-profile people." My stare doesn't waver.

"Yes, sir." He jots an address down on a piece of paper and slides it across the desk.

I pick it up and read it. She's going back to her friend's place.

"Thanks," I say, and peel off a few Ben Franklins. "For your trouble. My five-star review will be online in a few days." I hand him Grant's keys and write down my parents' phone number on a notepad. "Can you call this number and let them know their car is here? Tell them thanks for letting me borrow it."

I can't help it. I just fucking can't. I give the concierge a shit-eating grin. "It was a sweet ride."

CHAPTER TWENTY-ONE

I get a speeding ticket on my way back to the city.

Fine, I get two tickets, but I'm in a hurry in case Pink does something like load her luggage onto a train and move back upstate before I can get to her. She's no longer employed, no longer wants me, so there's nothing stopping her from going back to her parents.

Fear crashes through me.

I can't lose Pink. Since I met her, my life has had more meaning than ever before. My life has been fuller. More substantive.

After the way my family has treated her and her family, she has no reason whatsoever to trust me. No reason to give me another chance. But I have to try because she's everything to me.

It takes me for-fucking-ever to find a parking spot in her friend's neighborhood, but I finally slide my Tesla between a Prius and a Charger. I take the steps to the door of her building two at a time and ring the buzzer.

No answer.

Doesn't surprise me. Pink is so savvy that she either figured I'd follow her, or she doesn't want to see anyone at all right now.

I wait until a thirtyish couple leaves the building, chattering and cuddling, and I grab the door before it closes. I skip up the stairs like lightning until I hit the landing on the second floor, turn right, and stop in front of her friend's door. I knock.

Nothing.

I ring the bell.

Still nothing.

I pound on the door.

Fuck me. I get no response at all.

At this point, I'm not proud. I stoop to putting my ear against the door to make sure no one's home.

No sound whatsoever. I've missed her.

I have a few options. One—check my place. Two—swing by Checkmate HQ. Three—go to 7th Inning Stretch and get shitfaced because I've screwed up so badly that I'm probably going to be alone for the rest of my sorry life.

I trot down the stairs. I don't know where Pink has gone, but I do know that if I don't find her before she leaves the city, I'm down for a nice long drive upstate where I'm sure she'll end up because that's where her support system is. Family is everything to Pink, so they're the ones she'll go to.

My heart crumbles again. I should be the one she'd go to when she needs support.

When I do find her, I need something to prove my loyalty. Something to prove I wasn't helping my parents with their ridiculous plot. Something with meaning to prove how much I do love her and want her in my life more than anything else in this world.

I'm ambling down the last few stairs when an idea springs to life, and I stop.

Something with meaning. Something that will have meaning for Pink and me both.

Warmth spreads through my chest, and a smile turns up my lips.

My idea is either going to be the most brilliant gesture of devotion that will send Pink flying into my arms, or it will be the stupidest mistake that will mark me for life. Not sure which, but Pink is worth the risk.

I pull out my phone as I leave the building and stroll to my car. I Google the tattoo parlor where Leo, Dex, and I got our tattoos years ago when we first went into business and Ava—aspiring graphic artist—designed our company logo. Riding high on the excitement of starting our company, we got hammered and stumbled into a tattoo shop.

A few hours later, the three of us walked out inked.

After typing in the name of the shop, I hit enter, and voilà. It's still in business.

Thirty minutes later, I'm sitting in a chair in that shop.

"You sure, man?" The artist, who has tats covering every square inch of real estate on his body, eyes me. He's got a fresh drill in his gloved hand, and his long Garibaldi beard and slick, shiny head make him look as badass as any nightclub bouncer I've ever seen.

"Let's do this thing," I say on a small laugh. It's the phrase Pink has used to help me tackle some tough stuff lately.

The tattoo artist shakes his head, fires up the drill, and goes to work on my arm. "Your dime and your skin."

Says the man with an opening zipper tattooed along the center of his head, red brains inked where the zipper teeth part.

While he's working on me, I text Dex.

How's Chloe?

His reply is instantaneous.

Dude...

I know my partner better than I know myself, and that means things are bad.

Is she okay?

The dots jump, then Dex's message pops onto the screen.

There was no time for meds. The nurse came out a second ago and said the baby is crowning. I'm glad I'm a guy.

I laugh. Women are definitely tougher than men.

I send Dex one last message.

Keep me posted.

When the tattoo artist is done, I pay the man and step out onto the sidewalk. It's late Saturday night. New York City is zinging with energy, the people walking past in both directions are pumped and excited. I breathe in the warm night air as horns honk and a city bus rumbles by, billowing out exhaust.

I try Pink's cell, but she doesn't answer. I swing by HQ, but her desk is cleaned out. I stop by her friend's apartment one more time, but no one answers. I go to my place. Her things are gone, and my house key is on the credenza in the entryway.

I plop down on the sofa. Strange that this place doesn't feel like home anymore now that Pink is gone. I've looked everywhere I know to look. I'll make the rounds again tomorrow, and if I don't find her, I'll take a drive upstate.

Fuck it, I can't handle the silence. Silence didn't bother me a few weeks ago. But now? Now it sucks balls. I roll up my sleeve, take a picture of the new artwork on my arm, and text it to Pink with a message: *I really do love you.*

Shitfaced it is.

I call an Uber to take me to 7th Inning Stretch so I can drink myself into the gutter, where I obviously belong because I'm scum. I've hurt Pink and my family has messed with hers in the worst possible way.

While I'm waiting for my ride, my phone dings.

It's a text from Dex.

Mommy and baby boy are doing well. May be able to go home tomorrow. We're staying in the Hamptons so we can drive them back to the city.

I smile at the phone, then return the message.

Tell the proud parents congrats. I'll be waiting at their apartment when you get back. Tonight I'm going to 7th Inning to celebrate for them.

I might as well. There's nothing to celebrate in my own miserable life. And my time with Pink has shown me how much I don't want to be alone.

CHAPTER TWENTY-TWO

I'm drowning my sorrows in a tequila shot when Jacob Rush, bartender extraordinaire and co-owner of 7th Inning Stretch, dries his hands on a towel and steps over to me.

"What's up, buddy?" He leans against the bar across from me.

I grumble under my breath and knock back my second shot of Patrón. "Hit me again."

Jacob studies me as he pours me another. "Lose a chess match or something?" He busts my chops.

Since he and his jock buddies took me, Leo, and Dex under their wings in college and helped us transform into muscular men who can hold our own at the gym as well as we can over a chess board, I let it go. "Something like that." I outmaneuvered my father, but I still lost my girl.

She willingly put herself at my mercy. Made herself vulnerable. And I let her get hurt.

I roll up my sleeve and show Jacob my new tat. It's red and puffy and swollen.

"Wow. Were you drunk?" he asks.

"Hell no." I down another shot. "But I'm gonna be pretty soon." I roll my finger in a *keep the shots coming* gesture.

"Maybe you should slow down," Jacob says.

"Maybe you should shut up." I give it right back to him.

He knows I'm an asshole and he's still my friend, so he can handle my foul mood.

It's getting late and it's Saturday night, which means the crowd will only grow thicker until Last Call. It's New York City, after all —the city that never sleeps.

Jacob motions to someone over my head and waves them over. Then he pours a drink for the three people sitting to my right. "On the house. Mind vacating these seats?"

The people swipe their fifteen dollar drinks off the bar, thank Jacob, and wander away.

Ethan Wilde—whom we love to call Lunkhead just to irritate him since he owns the gym we all frequent—takes one of the stools, along with his fiancée, Adeline.

"Oh, yay. Another happy couple," I say like an ass. Seriously, they seem to be multiplying. *Everyone* I flipping know is happy and getting married and...

I knock back the liquid gold in my shot glass and slam it down on the bar.

I don't miss the look Jacob shoots at Ethan as he nods at my new tat. Ethan leans over to take a gander at the new work on my forearm.

"Wow. How much tequila had you consumed when you did that?" Ethan makes the same assumption Jacob did when he first saw it.

"Fuck you," I say.

He chuckles and slaps me on the back. It's a total dude gesture to let me know he's there for me. "Fuck you, too, buddy."

Jacob is already pouring Ethan and Adeline their favorite drinks without them having to ask. Ethan gets a Guinness while Adeline likes...I look at the foo-foo drink Jacob pours into a martini glass for her with an apple slice. No idea what it is, but it's obviously a drink that's off limits to anyone with high levels of testosterone.

"You make the best Appletinis in town, Jacob." Adeline lifts her glass in a toast. "To Chloe and Leo."

"Ah, word's already out," I say, lifting my glass for Jacob to fill it.

He does. "Last one, buddy."

"Bullshit." I toast with Adeline and Ethan. "To baby makes three." I'm happy for my partner and his lady, but it makes me feel like shit. Selfish, I know, but the toast only punctuates the hollowness I feel down to my soul.

"Dex has been texting everyone for Leo," Ethan says. "He said you'd be here celebrating for them."

Someone tries to take the third seat that Jacob ransomed from one of his customers.

"Seat's taken." Jacob shoos them away. He waves to a back corner of the bar.

When I turn around to see who Jacob is trying to lure into that vacant barstool, which he seems to be guarding with his life, it's Ethan's sister, Grace. She's ignoring him and is as far on the other side of the bar as she can get.

Uh oh. Either their *thing*—you know the little secret love affair I stumbled upon when I saw them together in Georgetown—is still going on, or Jacob *wants* it to still be going on. Not sure which, so I study the situation. Jacob, then Grace, then Jacob. She's ignoring him. His face is turning red.

Definitely Jacob still wants a thing with Grace, but she's clearly having none of it.

I feel Jacob's pain.

"Gimme another," I say to Jacob.

"No," he says, and fills a drink for another customer.

"Come on, man. I've had a hard day." I'm not beneath begging, and I've had just enough tequila already to do so. "I'll get down on my knees."

Jacob slides the drink across the counter, and the customer disappears into the crowd. "I might take you up on that if I were gay, but I'm not into dick," he deadpans without filling my shot glass.

"Very funny." I turn my glass upside down on the bar. "Thanks for nothin'."

"I'll have a sparkling water," a familiar voice says just behind me. It's velvety and sweet, and slides over my ears, sending blood pounding through my veins and making my heartrate speed.

I whirl around on my stool. "Pink." I'm dumbfounded. "You're here."

Gently, she knocks a knuckle against the side of my head. "Brilliant deduction, Einstein. I knew you were a genius, but *wow*."

Jacob, Ethan, and Adeline let out a friendly laugh, which I ignore.

My woman is here. Well, I'm not sure if she's still my woman, but the tender smile on her face makes a seed of hope spring to life in my chest. "How'd you find me?"

She glances around the crowded bar, but I swear, it's like me and Pink are the only people here. Everyone else fades. "Dex texted Leticia. Leticia texted me." Pink shrugs. "It was like the telephone game. I'm glad your location didn't get distorted as it went down the line, or I might've ended up in the Asian Massage & Stretch Parlor in Chinatown." Her brow furrows, but her eyes sparkle with humor. "I think that's the place I see on the news at least once a month that gets raided for delivering more services than just massages and stretching."

"I didn't know my brother was Hannah's father," I blurt. It's no secret by now that I'm not one to mince words, and that I'm not exactly a master at smooth conversation. The tequila has loosened my tongue even more, so there's that. "I won't let my parents bother you or your family anymore."

"Thank you," she whispers, taking a step closer. That one little step is the most promising thing I've seen in hours, and my pulse kicks. "How will that affect Checkmate?"

"I don't care," I spit out. "My partners and I have dodged a lot of bullets in our careers. We won't let this one take us down either." At least not without a fight. "We'll figure it out. We always do."

Her eyes glitter. Then they drop to my mouth, and her lips part as though she's thinking of...

Hot damn.

A burly guy who has obviously had far more tequila than me, bumps into Pink from behind. "Oh!" She stumbles toward me, and my arms open for her, as though it's the most natural, the most automatic thing in the world.

Because it is.

My arms circle her waist, and I pull her between my legs. She molds both palms to my chest. "Hi," she whispers.

Her warm, sweet breath washes over my skin, and I know I can never let this woman go. Not ever. Judging from the way she's getting comfy in my arms, I don't think it will come to stalking. Thank God.

"Why'd you come looking for me?" I ask. I have to know. Have to hear her say the words.

She looks down at my tat. "That has meaning. You wouldn't have done it if you weren't being honest."

"You believe me?" My heart races so fast I'm afraid it might burst from my chest like a scene straight out of *Alien*.

She reaches for my arm, tracing around the swollen, red design. "Anyone who would do this is telling the truth."

I throw my head back and laugh. "I guess it was kinda extreme." I look at the Checkmate logo inked into my arm. I had googly eyes and glasses added to the stallion. Next to it is the queen chess piece, also with glasses, and the name Pink scrawled through the base. Farther down my arm is a smaller chess piece—a pawn. It's got a Gerber baby curl on the top of its head. No name of course, but hopefully...

My gaze drops to her stomach. I press a gentle palm there and splay my fingers. "If not now, hopefully, someday. If you'll still have me."

She nods, her eyes sparkling with happiness.

I get lost in them.

She leans in and places a kiss on my cheek.

Nice.

Then her lips burn a trail to my ear.

Even nicer.

"I'll have you," she whispers against my ear, her warm breath sending shockwaves down my spine. "In every position you can think of."

I growl. I fucking *growl*. My fingers smooth up her neck to her jaw, where I trace the creamy skin with the pad of my thumb.

Her breath hitches.

Oh yeah. The tat is going to be so worth it.

"Get a room," Ethan says. He sends a wadded napkin sailing at my head.

"Best idea I've heard all night," I murmur against Pink's lips.

I slant my lips across hers and kiss her deep and lovingly until another wadded napkin hits the back of my head.

When we come up for air, her voice is breathy and soft. "Yep, great idea. I need privacy to show you *my* new artwork."

"You...you inked your virgin skin?" I swat her on the rump.

"Ouch!" she yelps. "Yes, after I got the picture of yours and the message you texted me. You just smacked it."

My head snaps back. "You tattooed your gorgeous ass?" My mind reels.

"Yep. Just for you." Her arms circle my neck.

I can't help it. I lick my lips. "I'd love to kiss it and make it better. What is it?"

"The word Oz and a pair of slippers." She shrugs. "But ruby slippers don't work for me, so they're pink."

I angle my head so it fits in the notch of her neck, and lightly bite her soft skin. "You had my name tattooed on the cheek of your ass?" I want to devour her right here and now. It's like she's branded herself just for me.

"Yes," she says with a blush. "So only you can see it."

For the first time in years, the pieces of my heart have fallen back into place, and it's whole again. "I can't wait to take a very close look." The sensual, needy tone of my voice holds a promise. A promise I know she's going to enjoy. For hours.

Naughtiness dances in her eyes. "Then let's go so I can show you."

EPILOGUE

It's standing room only at Oscar Wilde's. Kendall has pulled together an incredible party to announce our engagement.

Leo and Chloe have brought their newborn boy, who they've named Harvey. Magnus and Gerard are here, but they're leaving to go back overseas tomorrow. Poor guys are going to have jet lag for the next decade because of all the trips they're going to make between continents. They're part of our extended family, though, and wouldn't miss the special moments in our lives.

Leticia brought her husband, and I gotta say, that guy has his hands full...in a good way. She's even forgiven me for letting Pink leave the company, and she's been lining up interviews. I swear I'll make it work this time with whoever she hires.

Dex and Ava are here, and so are our college buddies we still hang with. Ethan Wilde hasn't left his fiancée's side. Jacob Rush and the other owners of 7th Inning Stretch seem to be stag tonight, but they're happy, laughing, and enjoying themselves.

The IPO is back on track, but we've narrowed our field of investors and uninvited the members who were cowed so easily by my father. We've decided not to release quite as many shares, which means we won't raise as much money for the expansion because we're holding on to more of the stock ourselves. In exchange, we're taking the expansion slower, so as not to chew up too much of Checkmate's capital. The best decision of all is we've added a female investor who will also be on the board. It seemed the best way to balance all the egos around the table during our board meetings.

Of course, Leo, Dex, and I are maintaining the lion's share of Checkmate Inc. stock. Once the threat posed by my father was over, we realized we weren't ready to give up so much control over our baby. We're still young and have a lot of hardworking years ahead of us. Checkmate doesn't have to conquer the world overnight. However, we've seen fit to reward those who've been with us from the beginning because loyalty like that is hard to find. Leticia, Magnus, and Gerard have been issued shares in their names, so they now have a stake in the company, too. They'll have a vote at the table, and the three of them will give us a deeper bench when it comes to the female perspective—Magnus and Gerard's words, not mine.

Our baby is in good hands and safe from corporate predators.

Speaking of a baby...

I look over the ocean of people, finally finding the person I want to see...touch...taste. When we're alone, of course. Pink is talking to her mom, her dad, sister, and niece over by the champagne fountain the restaurant has set up at the end of the long bar. It's still too soon to tell if Pink is expecting, but if she isn't, it'll happen in time. We certainly go at it enough. I make my way through the crowd, greeting people as I go. When I finally reach Pink, I snake an arm around her waist.

"Having a good time?" I ask her family. I guess they're my family now, too, and that makes my heart expand so much that I'm not sure my chest is big enough to hold it anymore.

Hannah holds out her hands to me, and I take her in my arms.

Avery looks at Mr. and Mrs. Tate with a noticeable amount of uncertainty. They nod at her.

"Your parents sent me a letter," Avery says.

I stiffen.

"They dropped the custody suit." She chews her lip. "And they apologized. They never knew about..." She glances at her daughter.

I nod so she doesn't have to say the rest out loud in front of Hannah.

Grant finally fessed up and told my parents everything. My father probably had to bribe it out of him with money...or a Lamborghini, but at least Mom and Dad know the whole truth now. Avery never denied Grant visitation, which was the excuse he used for not telling anyone about Hannah. Avery doesn't have a drug addiction and never did. Those were lies Grant made up so Dad wouldn't come down on him.

What a twat.

Avery looks around, fidgeting with her glass. She's clearly nervous. "Will they be here tonight?"

I shake my head. "Absolutely not." They've asked forgiveness from me and Kendall, too, and promised to try and change so they can be part of our lives. Part of their grandchildren's lives. Hopefully, we'll get there one day, but it's going to take a long time and a lot of changing for them to earn back my trust.

The upside of the whole mess is that my dad is finally accepting that Grant really is a gigantic douche. And my mom is finally accepting that she's got to set boundaries with my father. Baby steps, but they are positive baby steps, so that's a win-win.

"Oh!" I pretend that I'd forgotten the legal papers in my back pocket. With little Hannah in my arms, I don't want to reach for them. I'm still a little insecure about holding a child, so I turn to the side and ask Pink, "There's something in my back pocket. Can you get it?"

The gigantic, pear-shaped diamond I put on her finger glitters under the lights. She wanted something less...I think ostentatious was the word she used, but I would have none of that. The way she permanently inked her ass with my name is for my eyes only. The ring announces to the world that she's mine.

Pink pulls the documents out of my pocket, her forehead wrinkling.

"A little something for Avery and Hannah," I say.

The lines in Pink's forehead deepen.

I give her a warm smile that says *it's all good,* so she gives the papers to her sister.

When Avery unfolds them and skims the contents, her eyes round, and her head snaps up to gawk at me.

"That was my trust fund, which I don't need. It's Hannah's now." Not only will it cover her hearing problems, but she'll be taken care of like a princess for the rest of her life. It seemed only right that some of the Randolph money go to one of their own. Coming from me, Avery won't have to worry about the money having strings.

Pink gasps. "Oscar."

I angle my body so Hannah and I are closer to Pink. I wink at her.

She kisses me on the cheek, but then her hand slips behind me so that her parents can't see, and she pinches one of *those* cheeks.

I love it.

From the corner of my eye, I see Sean Montgomery and Zach Simmons walk in with their dates.

"Oh!" I say again, like I'm just now remembering another important detail. "Can you take Hannah for a minute?" I ask Avery. "There's someone I want Kendall to meet."

Hannah goes to her mother, and I lace my fingers with Pink's. "Come with me." I lead her over toward Sean. When he glances in my direction, I notch my chin so he'll join us.

"Sean, this is Kendall Tate," I say.

"Congratulations," he says to me. Then he turns to Pink and says, "My condolences. Oz is definitely getting the better end of the deal." He winks. "Nice to meet you, Kendall. I hear you're an experienced event planner."

She nods. "I am." Then she frowns. "Or I was."

"Sean's company organizes the Annual Weekend Warrior event and a whole lotta other events around the city." I smile at Pink.

She looks from me to Sean, understanding dawning in her intelligent eyes.

"I have an opening if you're available for an interview," Sean says.

She snuggles into my side. "I happen to be unemployed, so yes, I'm available."

He hands Pink his card. "Call my office, and we'll set something up."

I point him in the direction of the booze, and he's gone.

"I'm assuming you pulled some strings?" Kendall says, and I know where she's going. She likes to do things on her own. Be independent. Earn her own way.

Exactly like me.

"Only for the interview." I get serious. "The rest is up to you, but I have no doubt you'll knock his socks off." I run my finger along her nose. "Speaking of knocking someone's socks off..." I lean back and let my gaze coast over her sleek black dress that molds to her gorgeous figure. It redefines the term *little black dress.* "Since that dress isn't covering much of your prime real estate, I'd like to peel it off you, along with everything else." My stare drops to her black strappy heels. "You're not wearing socks, which will save me some time."

She pinches my shoulder. "We're in public."

My gaze flits around the crowded restaurant. "They won't miss us if we disappear to my car for a bit."

"Do you ever think of anything but getting me naked?" she asks.

I chuckle. "Right now, I'm thinking about a lot of other things." Things I'll do to her *after* I get her naked. I lean down and whisper the dirties, filthiest things in her ear.

A shiver races over her, and a tiny gasp slips through her lips.

When I finish, I straighten and look into her eyes.

They gleam with desire, and warmth floods my chest.

"That's...that's..." Her voice is breathy with need, and she can't finish her sentence.

I finish it for her. "Sinful?"

She nods. "Meet me at the car." The extra sway in her hips draws my attention like a magnet.

I wait until she disappears through the front door. And I follow.

* * *

Thank you for reading SINFUL GAMES, the fourth book in my Checkmate Inc. series of standalone novels. There will be more stories for the sexy, alpha guys who are associated with Checkmate Inc.

In the meantime, try my DARE ME Series. Set on the picturesque vacation island of Angel Fire Falls. The three smokin' hot Remington Brothers are back in town, and they're sexier than ever.

Sign up for my VIPeep Reader List to find out about new books, awesome giveaways, and exclusive content including excerpts and deleted scenes: SHELLY'S VIPEEP READER LIST

I pinky swear to never, ever share your email addy with anyone, and I only send out newsletters when I've got exciting news about a sale, a new book, or awesome giveaways.

About DARE ME ONCE, the first book in this new series:

Love is a risk worth taking in this sizzling romance about secrets and second chances...

Scarlett Devereaux's life on the Gulf Coast went from riches to rags so scandalously fast that she barely had time to kiss her Jimmy Choos goodbye. Now, with a new alias (Lily Barns), a new budget (tighter than a pair of Spanx), and a new job on the vacation island of Angel Fire Falls, she's daring to reinvent herself.

Single dad Trace Remington is devoted first and foremost to raising his young son, who has Asperger's. With flying his float-plane and salvaging his family's island resort too, he has time for little else. His brothers think he needs a break from his all-work-no-play lifestyle, so they goad him into action. In response to their dare, Trace asks a sexy tourist for her number, only to discover afterward that she's the resort's brilliant new hospitality manager.

The sparks of flirtation soon ignite into a flame too hot to ignore. But Lily and Trace both have pasts that threaten to tear them apart. Now, they'll need to admit their secrets to each other...or risk ending their relationship before it really begins.

One-Click DARE ME ONCE!

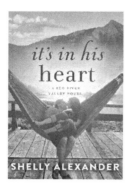

And don't miss my steamy Best-selling IT'S IN HIS... Series. Set in a quirky but gorgeous mountain town in the southern Rockies where the nights are cool and the romance is hot.

Read book 1, IT'S IN HIS HEART, now!

Reviews are an author's best friend! They spread the word to others who enjoy the same books as you. So be sure to leave a review for SINFUL GAMES on AMAZON, B&N, GOODREADS, BOOKBUB and any other favorite sites.

ALSO BY

SHELLY ALEXANDER

The Red River Valley Series

It's In His Heart – Coop & Ella's Story

It's In His Touch – Blake & Angelique's Story

It's In His Smile – Talmadge & Miranda's Story

It's In His Arms – Mitchell & Lorenda's Story

It's In His Forever – Langston & His Secret Love's Story

It's In His Song – Dylan & Hailey's Story (2019)

The Angel Fire Falls Series

Dare Me Once – Trace & Lily's Story

Dare Me Again – Elliott & Rebel's Story

Dare Me Now – To be announced

Dare Me Always – To be announced

The Checkmate Inc. Series

ForePlay – Leo & Chloe's Story

Rookie Moves – Dex & Ava's Story

Get Wilde – Ethan & Adeline's Story

Sinful Games – Oz & Kendall's Story

Wilde Rush – Jacob & Grace's Story Coming 2019

ACKNOWLEDGMENTS

Thank you to my friends, Dave and Karen, for lending your Wall Street experience and knowledge of public stock offerings for this book. Your input was invaluable.

I owe much gratitude to Jo Swinney and her network of super bloggers for always supporting my work and for getting the word out about my books. I love you!

And as always, thank you to my lovely readers. As I write this book, my husband and son are delivering laptops, school supplies, and toys to an orphanage in India, which I've been able to donate because you've seen fit to spend your hard-earned money on my books. You are lovely in my eyes.

ABOUT THE AUTHOR

Shelly Alexander is the author of contemporary romances that are sometimes sweet, sometimes sizzling, and always sassy. She is an Amazon Bestseller in multiple categories and in multiple countries. Her debut novel, *It's In His Heart*, was a 2014 Golden Heart® finalist.

Shelly grew up traveling the world, earned a BBA in marketing, and worked in the business world for twenty-five years. With four older brothers, she and her sister watched every *Star Trek* episode ever made, joined the softball team instead of ballet class, and played with G.I. Joes while the Barbie Corvette stayed tucked in the closet. When she had three sons of her own, she decided to escape her male-dominated world by reading romance novels and has been hooked ever since. Now she spends her days writing steamy contemporary romances while tending to two toy poodles named Mozart and Midge.

Be the first to know about Shelly's new releases, giveaways, appearances, and bonus scenes not included in her books! Sign up for her newsletter and receive VIP treatment:

http://shellyalexander.net

Other ways to stalk Shelly:
BookBub

Amazon
Email

[f] facebook.com/ShellyAlexanderAuthor

[t] twitter.com/ShellyCAlexande

[o] instagram.com/shellycalexander

Made in the USA
Columbia, SC
16 June 2019